The Haunted Baronet

A Gothic Horror Tale of Sin, Secrets, and Supernatural Consequences

A Modern Translation

Adapted for the Contemporary Reader

J. Sheridan Le Fanu

Translated by Tim Zengerink

Table of Contents

Preface - Message to the Reader

What If You Could Help Rebuild the Greatest Library in Human History?

Thousands of years ago, the Library of Alexandria stood as the crown jewel of human achievement — a sanctuary where the collected wisdom of every known civilization was gathered, preserved, and shared freely.

And then, it was lost.

Through fire, conquest, and the slow erosion of time, humanity lost not just books — but ideas, dreams, discoveries, and stories that could have changed the world forever.

Today, the Library of Alexandria lives again — and you are invited to be a part of its restoration.

Our mission is simple yet profound:

To rebuild the greatest library the world has ever known, and to translate all timeless works into every language and dialect, so that no seeker of knowledge is ever left behind again.

By joining our movement to rebuild the modern Library of Alexandria, you become part of an unprecedented mission:

- **Unlimited Access to the Greatest Audiobooks & eBooks Ever Written:**

  Instantly explore thousands of legendary works—Plato, Shakespeare, Jane Austen, Leo Tolstoy, and countless more. All instantly available to read or listen, placing a complete literary universe at your fingertips.

- **Beautiful Paperback & Deluxe Editions at Printing Cost**

  Own any title as an elegant paperback, deluxe hardcover, or stunning collectible boxset—offered to you at true printing cost, delivered straight to your door. Build your personal Library of Alexandria, crafted for beauty, built for durability, and worthy of proud display.

- **Fresh Translations for Modern Readers—in Every Language & Dialect**

  Enjoy timeless masterpieces reimagined in clear, contemporary language—no more outdated phrases or obscure references. Alongside the original versions, we're tirelessly translating these classics into every language and dialect imaginable, ensuring accessibility and understanding across cultures and generations.

- **Join a Global Renaissance of Literature & Knowledge**

  You directly support expanding our library, publishing deluxe editions at true cost, translating works into all global languages, and bringing humanity's greatest stories to people everywhere. By joining today, you're not just preserving a legacy of masterpieces; you set in motion a powerful wave of literary accessibility.

Become a Torchbearer of Knowledge.

Join us for free now at **LibraryofAlexandria.com**

Together, we will ensure that the light of human wisdom never fades again.

With gratitude and a shared love of knowledge,

The Modern Library of Alexandria Team

Visit:

www.libraryofalexandria.com

Or scan the code below:

Introduction

Ancestral Sins, Haunted Lineages,
and the Burden of Unseen Guilt

J. Sheridan Le Fanu's The Haunted Baronet, first published in 1871 as part of his collection Chronicles of Golden Friars, is one of the most layered and symbolically charged entries in his extensive body of supernatural fiction. While not as well known as Carmilla or Green Tea, this novella weaves together many of Le Fanu's most enduring themes: generational guilt, spectral retribution, buried secrets, and the psychological decay of the aristocracy. Through a ghost story that unfolds across both the social and the spiritual realms, Le Fanu creates a richly gothic meditation on the inescapability of the past.

Set in the fictional English village of Golden Friars, the tale centers on the ominous figure of Sir Bale Mardykes, the titular baronet who returns to his ancestral home after years abroad. Cold, austere, and generally despised by his neighbors, Sir Bale becomes the target of suspicion when a series of strange occurrences begin to unfold— disappearances, visions, inexplicable noises, and, above all, the persistent sense that the family's long history is catching up with him. The nearby lake, known for its ancient superstitions and rumored hauntings, plays a central role in the unfolding drama, becoming both a symbol and a literal gateway for the spectral forces that surround Mardykes Hall.

What makes The Haunted Baronet particularly compelling is Le Fanu's focus on moral and psychological decay. Sir Bale is not a raving villain, but a man hardened by isolation and guilt—one whose icy demeanor masks deeper, unacknowledged fears. As the story progresses, it becomes clear that his family's legacy is one of quiet cruelty, cloaked in social propriety and buried beneath generational denial. The ghosts that haunt the baronet are not random—they are consequences. They arise not just from what he has done, but from what his forebears never accounted for.

This introduction will examine the structure, themes, and enduring literary significance of The Haunted Baronet. We will explore how Le Fanu builds tension through atmosphere, how he uses the landscape itself as a character of menace, and how the story fits within the larger tradition of Victorian ghost literature. Most importantly, we'll analyze the novella's moral and metaphysical implications—how Le Fanu crafts a narrative that is not merely about the supernatural, but about what it means to live under a shadow that will not lift. This is a story of haunting, yes—but haunting as inheritance, as memory, as fate.

The Landscape of Guilt:
Mardykes Hall and the Spirit of the Lake

From its earliest pages, The Haunted Baronet evokes a mood of oppressive quiet. Golden Friars may appear idyllic on the surface, but it is a village saturated with superstition and silence. The lake, in particular, takes on a mythic quality—its still waters reflecting more than sky, its depths whispered to conceal more than fish. This natural setting is not just backdrop; it is integral to the horror. The environment holds memory. It resists forgetting.

Le Fanu makes it clear that Mardykes Hall is a place where things have happened—things not spoken of, but deeply felt. The villagers, though deferential to Sir Bale due to class and custom, treat him with visible discomfort. They sense, as the reader does, that something unwholesome surrounds the estate. The lake becomes a character in its own right—a place of mystery, rumor, and power. It has seen too much. It holds the secrets of the Mardykes family, and its waters act almost as a conscience, waiting to rise.

This use of landscape as psychic territory is classic Le Fanu. In The Familiar, it is the streets of Dublin that close in. In Uncle Silas, it is the decaying manor and its locked doors. In The Haunted Baronet, it is the lake that remembers. And within that lake lies the key to the family's legacy of hidden sin. A boating accident—perhaps a murder—lingers at the heart of the tale. The specifics are obscured, just as they would be in real life, but the emotional truth is sharp: someone died unjustly, and the water will not forget.

Sir Bale, meanwhile, stands at the edge of this watery memory, both physically and symbolically. He visits the lake. He watches it. He seems drawn to it as one would be drawn to a confessional. But he does not speak. He does not admit. And in that silence, the haunting grows.

The Ghost as Heirloom:
Inheritance, Class, and Repetition

In many of Le Fanu's stories, the supernatural is deeply moral. Not moralistic—but bound to moral consequence. His ghosts are not demons or random spirits—they are the echoes of ethical failure, and in The Haunted Baronet, the ghost is not just a figure from the past— it is the past itself, manifest. What makes the story chilling is that its horror is embedded in continuity. The sins of the father—and the grandfather, and the great-grandfather—have not vanished. They have been passed down like property, like titles, like land.

Sir Bale inherits more than a house. He inherits a debt, a psychic weight. And because he neither acknowledges nor atones for that inheritance, it begins to consume him. This dynamic turns the ghost into something far more than a plot device. It becomes a kind of spiritual parasite, feeding on denial, growing stronger in the absence of confession. The haunting intensifies not because of some incantation or trespass, but because the truth remains unspoken.

This concept of inherited guilt was particularly potent in the Victorian era, when questions of class, empire, and moral responsibility loomed large. Le Fanu, writing from a Protestant Anglo-Irish perspective, understood the complexities of legacy. His aristocrats are never merely decadent—they are haunted, not just by ghosts, but by the knowledge that their position is built on quiet violence. The Mardykes family, like many noble houses in gothic fiction, stands as a metaphor for systems that are both powerful and rotting from within.

In this context, the ghost in The Haunted Baronet is not just an avenger—it is an accuser. Its presence is proof that the past is never past. And its refusal to disappear is a reminder that inheritance is not always a gift. Sometimes, it is a curse—especially when what is inherited is the burden of silence.

Le Fanu's Moral Vision
and the Enduring Power of the Unresolved

As with many of his best works, Le Fanu refuses to offer easy closure in The Haunted Baronet. The haunting is not neatly resolved. The ghost is not banished. And the baronet does not repent. Instead, the story ends with a kind of emotional and narrative ambiguity that heightens its impact. Sir Bale's fate is sealed not by a climactic confrontation, but by his own inability to change. He is not destroyed by the ghost. He is destroyed by the meaning of the ghost—by what it represents, by what he refuses to face.

This approach makes The Haunted Baronet more than a gothic melodrama. It is a story about the weight of memory, about the consequences of unspoken crimes and the way evil lingers not just in places, but in families, in legacies, in names. The baronet is not evil in the conventional sense. He is cold, isolated, and prideful. But those qualities, in Le Fanu's moral universe, are enough to let darkness in.

The brilliance of Le Fanu lies in his ability to let the supernatural feel inevitable. He does not over-explain. He does not overplay. He builds a world in which the ghost is always nearby—not because it wants to scare, but because it cannot leave until something is acknowledged. In that sense, The Haunted Baronet is a story of failed absolution. The opportunity to confess, to break the cycle, is present—but it is ignored. And the cycle continues.

This structure influenced countless later writers—from Henry James to Shirley Jackson to Sarah Waters—authors who understood that ghost stories are most powerful not when they show the ghost, but when they show what the ghost means. In The Haunted Baronet, the ghost is not a horror—it is a truth.

A truth that the living will do anything to avoid.

And that, precisely, is why it returns.

With The Haunted Baronet, Le Fanu offers one of his most layered, haunting, and morally resonant works. It is not just a ghost story—it is a tale of legacy, of conscience, and of the cost of silence passed down through generations. It reminds us that the worst hauntings are not always the loudest. They are the ones we inherit. And carry. And refuse to name.

Chapter I.
The George and Dragon

The small town of Golden Friars sat quietly beside a lake, surrounded by tall purple mountains, streaked with deep valleys and glowing with color. On some nights, when the moon was shining, the town looked like something from a dream—its old stone houses with steep roofs and narrow windows shining like silver, the church tower still ringing the curfew bell, and the tall black elm trees casting still shadows on the grass. It was one of the most beautiful and unusual places I'd ever seen.

From a distance, it almost looked like the town had been magically painted into the misty night air—so delicate and perfect it could vanish with a breeze.

On a peaceful summer night, the moonlight lit up the front of the George and Dragon, the town's cozy old inn made of gray stone. It had one of the best inn signs in all of England—a grand painting of St. George and the dragon, framed with fancy black iron and touches of gold, hanging between two large posts. It faced the lake, with the road running just in front of its door.

Inside the inn, a few of the regulars had gathered in the large sitting room to relax after the day. The room had dark wood walls and a warm fire burning, since the night air was a little chilly. The fire, mostly made of wood, gave the room a soft glow without making it too hot.

Doctor Torvey was there—a cheerful, round man who knew everyone's health problems and favorite remedies. He liked to laugh, smoke his pipe, and drink a glass of punch with a twist of lemon around this time each night. Sitting next to him was Mr. Peers, a thin, kind old man who had lived in India for over thirty years and still wore a pigtail—the last man in town to do so. Across from them was Jack Amerald, a retired navy captain with a wooden leg beside his real one propped on a chair. He drank grog, shouted like a sailor, and called everyone "hearties." In the center, near the fire, sat Tom Hollar. Though he was deaf, he always looked peaceful while he smoked his pipe and watched the flames. Every now and then, the innkeeper, Mr. Turnbull, would walk in, sit in the tall wooden chair, and join the conversation like everyone else. The inn had always been a friendly and equal place.

"So Sir Bale is finally coming back," said the doctor. "Heard anything new?"

"Not much," replied Mr. Turnbull. "Just that it's definitely true. The old place won't feel so empty anymore."

"They say the estate's deep in debt now, don't they?" asked the doctor in a low voice, giving a knowing wink.

"Well, they say he hasn't done much for years. I'll tell you that, just between us. But he'll sort it out eventually."

"He's better off saving money here than where he was," said the doctor with another serious nod.

"He's doing the smart thing," said Mr. Peers, letting out a stream of smoke. "And it's admirable if he's coming back to cut costs. Maybe he'll even get married. That's even more impressive if he dislikes the place as much as they say."

Then he smiled a little and went back to his pipe.

"They say he doesn't like it here—at least, he didn't," added the innkeeper.

"He hates it," said the doctor with another grim nod.

"No surprise, if what I've heard is true," said Captain Amerald. "Didn't he drown a woman and her child in the lake?"

"Hey! Don't go saying that out loud," said the doctor. "You're talking nonsense."

"By heaven," said the innkeeper in a shocked whisper, holding his pipe and staring wide-eyed, "I rent the house up there. Thank God we're alone in here!"

Captain Amerald placed his real foot on the floor, keeping his wooden leg resting, and glanced around the room.

"Well, if it wasn't him, then it was someone. I know something happened near Mardykes. I charted the spot myself—from Glads Scaur to Mardykes Jetty and from the George and Dragon sign down to that white house under Forrick Fells. Someone here told me exactly where they saw the body. I could swear I remember it. But no boat could ever reach it. That was strange, you know. I even wrote it in my logbook."

"Aye, Captain, folks have been talking nonsense like that," said Turnbull. "People love to gossip. But it was about his grandfather, not him. And I'd be in big trouble down here if people thought rumors like that were going around at the George and Dragon."

"Well, his grandfather or him—it wouldn't matter much to him, I suppose."

"There was never any proof, Captain. Just talk—nothing more. And the family up at Mardykes wouldn't even let a king speak that way about them. The ones who had a real reason to be angry about it have been dead for years, but anyone with their name still takes it seriously. And Sir Bale? He cares just as much as any of them. Not that I've got anything to worry about personally—people say he's a bit grumpy and not the best-looking, but as long as I keep paying rent, he can't kick me out of the George—not for another nine hundred and ninety-nine years, by the lease! A man has plenty of time to cool down by then. Still, it doesn't help to argue with touchy people. He could help this place—or hurt it—and there's no point upsetting him over something that happened long before he was even born. Isn't that right, Doctor?"

The Doctor, who also had to be careful in his business, nodded. "That's true, Dick. But still, it's an old story—older than either of us."

"And best left forgotten," Turnbull added quickly.

"Yes, best forgotten—but the trouble is, it won't be," said the Doctor, growing a bit braver. "Our friend the Captain here's already heard it, and the mistake he made proves it. The only thing worse than a story like that being remembered is when it's only half remembered. You can't stop people from talking. Stories like that outlive us all."

"Now that I think about it," said the Captain, "it was Dick Harman who told me—he's got the boat down there, an old sailor like me. I was out fishing for pike, and he rowed me over the spot. That's when I first heard the tale. Say, Tom—bring us another glass of brandy, will you?" he called as the waiter walked by. Then he clapped his good leg back on the chair beside his wooden one, which he liked to call his "jury-mast."

"I believe that story's going to be told long after we're gone," said Turnbull. "But I don't care much about the tale—just so long as they don't blame the wrong man." He tapped his glass with a spoon to signal Tom to bring him more punch. "And I think Sir Bale could be a good friend to this inn. I don't see why not. The George and Dragon's been in my family since King Charles the Second's time. Back then, it was William Turnbull who took the lease from Sir Tony Mardykes. They weren't baronets then—that came later during King George the

Second's reign. You can even look it up in the list of noble families. William came from London and rebuilt the stables— they were falling apart, just like it says in the lease. And ever since then, this place has always had the same name—the George and Dragon—and always been run by a Turnbull. That's known across England."

A few murmurs of agreement came from the group.

"We've always been churchgoers, brewed good drinks, and had a solid reputation, here and beyond. And as long as we pay the rent, no one can push us out. We've got as much right to this place—the inn, the fields, the croft, and the pasture—as Sir Bale has to that big house up there. So what the Mardykes think of me doesn't bother me— though they've always been good neighbors, and I'd like to keep it that way."

"Well said, Dick!" said Doctor Torvey. "I agree with you. And since it's just us here, and we're all friends, and you're your own boss—come on, tell us that story about the drowned woman, the way your father told it."

"Yes, do—and keep the drinks coming, my friend!" said the Captain.

Mr. Peers nodded with interest, while deaf Mr. Hollar, who hadn't been following the conversation, sat quietly smoking his pipe—like part of the furniture.

Turnbull took a sip of his punch and looked around. The door was shut, the fire was glowing warmly, the punch smelled sweet, and every face around him was friendly. So he said:

"Well, gentlemen, since you're asking, I don't see the harm in it. And at least this way there won't be any confusion. It happened more than ninety years ago. My father was just a boy, but he told me the story many times—right here in this very room."

He looked into his glass and stirred his drink slowly, lost in thought.

Chapter II.
The Drowned Woman

"It's not much of a tale," said the innkeeper at the George, "and I won't keep you long with it, gentlemen. There was a beautiful young woman named Miss Mary Feltram of Cloostedd. She was the last of her family, and they'd become very poor. The house is just ruins now—grass growing inside, ivy climbing the walls. No one's seen smoke from those chimneys in years. It's across the lake, surrounded by old trees, near the pass under Maiden Fells. You can spot it through a spyglass from the boat dock at Mardykes Hall."

"I've been there plenty of times," said the Doctor.

"Well, the Feltrams and Mardykes had dealings. Like any family, there was good and bad in both. But the Mardykes back then were a wild bunch. When old Feltram of Cloostedd died, his daughter was left in the care of Sir Jasper Mardykes. That was a bad day for her, poor girl. He was over twenty years older than her, and not the kind anyone could easily love—small, gloomy, and sour-faced."

"'Dow' means gloomy," the Doctor explained to the Captain.

"They say there was a magic ring in the Mardykes family—a bloodstone ring with some kind of spell on it. However it happened, the poor girl fell for him. Some say they got married, some say it was just talk, and never done properly by a priest. Either way, people talked, and she never left the house after that. They had two little children. She begged him to admit they were married, but he refused. He wouldn't even let the children use his last name. He was cold-hearted, stubborn, and went his own way. After he got tired of her, he wanted

15

to marry someone else—a lady from the Barnet family. So, the woman and her kids vanished from Mardykes Hall and were never seen there again. The oldest child, a boy, was left here at the George in my great-grandfather's care."

"That strange Philip Feltram who's been traveling with Sir Bale—is he from that family?" asked the Doctor.

"His grandson," said Mr. Peers, taking out his pipe. "The last of the line."

"No one knew what happened to the woman. Some said she moved far away, some said she went mad. Everyone had a different story. But the Mardykes never mentioned her or the children again. There was a man named Mr. Wigram who lived back then in Moultry—served in the navy, like the Captain here. One morning, he came to town for a boat, saying he'd seen something through his spyglass near Snakes Island—a woman in the water, up to her hips, holding a baby. He said she was stiff and upright. But when they went out in a boat to check, she was gone. The next day, he saw her again—and this time, the boatman saw her too. They rowed toward her as fast as they could, but after a mile, she vanished again.

Later, the vicar saw her. I forget his name now, but he was coming back from a funeral at Mortlock Church, with the sail up on the boat. As they passed Snakes Island, they suddenly heard a scream—high-pitched and chilling. It made their blood run cold. Then, about a hundred yards off, they saw her. She was pale as a ghost, her hair and face soaked, and she held the baby up to them. Her expression was cold and mocking. The boat came as close as it could, and the vicar reached out, trying to grab her. But she leaned in, holding the dead baby toward them—and then screamed so loudly it shook them to the bone. She disappeared in an instant. No living woman could rise out of the lake like that. Once they realized it, they knew it was a ghost. They prayed and sailed away fast—they wouldn't have faced that vision again for all the wealth of Mardykes Hall. Market folks later saw her in the same place, and ever since, no one wants to go near Snakes Island after dark."

"Do you know anything about that Feltram who's been traveling with Sir Bale?" the Doctor asked.

"They say he's not much good for anything—gentle but useless. A big awkward fool when he left here," said Turnbull. "The Feltrams and Mardykes were family once, which made what happened to that poor girl even worse. This young man is a descendant of the boy who was left here in my grandfather's care."

"Great-grandson," corrected Mr. Peers. "His father was the grandson. He served in the army and died in the West Indies. This Philip is the last of that family. He's considered illegitimate, of course, and what was left of the Feltram estate went to the Mardykes about eighty years ago. Sir Bale supports Philip now, and whatever people may say about the Mardykes, it's worth noting that this act is very kind."

"Agreed," said Turnbull.

While they talked, a horn sounded, and the mail coach pulled up outside the George and Dragon to drop off a passenger and some luggage.

Dick Turnbull got up and bustled out to the hallway, with the Doctor following far enough to peek around the door. They saw several canvas-covered trunks being brought in by Tom and a young helper, carefully stacking them near the staircase. The Doctor, curious as he was, didn't go out to read the labels—it wouldn't have been proper for a man of his standing—but he would have, if he could've gotten away with it.

Chapter III.
Philip Feltram

The new guest had just stepped into the front hall of the George, and Doctor Torvey could hear him speaking quietly with Mr. Turnbull. Since the Doctor was considered an important figure in Golden Friars, he didn't want to be seen listening in. He gently closed the door and went back to his seat by the fire. Leaning closer to his friends, he whispered that someone new had arrived at the inn. He couldn't make out much, but guessed the man had asked for a private room—judging by how many trunks he brought, it looked like he could build a whole church with them.

"Don't be so sure it's not Sir Bale himself," said Captain Amerald. He would've followed the Doctor to the door to get a better look, but his wooden leg made too much noise to sneak around quietly.

"No chance," said the Doctor. "Charley Twyne hears everything. He gets letters nearly every day. There's no sign of Sir Bale coming before the tenth. I'd bet anything this is just a traveler passing through. I don't know what's taking Turnbull so long—he knows we're all curious to find out who the man is."

"Well, whoever he is, he won't bother us," the Captain replied. He caught deaf Mr. Hollar's eye, nodded toward the table, and mimed shaking dice. Hollar gave a sunny smile and nodded back. The Captain stood up, brought over the backgammon set, and the two of them started their game, the sound of the pieces tapping and rolling filling the room.

Hollar got lucky early and made a good move, which the Captain didn't take well. He muttered about Hollar's luck, teased his playing, and loudly complained to the others—as if Hollar, who couldn't hear a word, might respond. Just then, the door opened and Turnbull entered, leading the new guest into the room. He guided the man to a vacant chair near the far corner of the table, close to the fire.

The man came in slowly, moving with a kind of quiet nervousness. There was something in the way he carried himself that said he didn't feel like he belonged. He was tall and very thin, with a slight hunch in his shoulders. His long, pale face looked tired and sad, like someone who had been through too much.

He murmured a thank you to Turnbull and took his seat without drawing attention, glancing around the room in a shy way, almost as if he felt guilty for disturbing the peace.

Captain Amerald peeked at him from beneath his thick gray eyebrows, pretending to focus on his game. Meanwhile, the Doctor made a mental note of every detail of the man's outfit, planning to tell his wife about it later.

The man's clothes matched the gloomy look on his face. He wore a short black cloak, a tall felt hat that looked foreign, and shiny leather leggings that hugged his skinny legs. Altogether, his appearance reminded people of old drawings of Guy Fawkes.

None of the men in the room actually knew what Sir Bale looked like. The Doctor and Mr. Peers remembered him vaguely from years back, but this man didn't match their memory at all. People who had seen Sir Bale recently said he was short, dark, and carried himself with confidence. This man was the opposite—tall, pale, and nervous. He looked like someone who'd had a hard life, not someone used to power or respect.

The Doctor sneaked another glance at him, and their eyes met for a moment. The man was sipping tea—a drink hardly anyone ordered in that room—but he didn't look embarrassed. The Doctor took this as a sign it was okay to talk. He cleared his throat and spoke kindly.

"It's been cold lately," he said. "A fire like this is a nice thing to have, don't you think?"

The man gave a faint smile and nodded, looking into the flames with what seemed like real warmth.

"A lot of people come here to visit," the Doctor went on. "It's a lovely place. Have you been here before?"

"Yes, many years ago," the stranger said softly.

There was a brief silence.

"Places change slowly, at least in the little things," said the Doctor, still trying to keep the conversation going. "And people do too. Populations shift. There's an old fellow we all meet in the end—his name's Death."

"And another old fellow called the Doctor who helps him along," joked the Captain, jumping in with a loud laugh.

"We're expecting someone to return soon who'll probably be an important figure in our small town," said the Doctor, ignoring the Captain's joke. "I mean Sir Bale Mardykes. His home, Mardykes Hall, looks beautiful from across the lake—it's a big, impressive old house."

The quiet stranger gave a slight nod, but it seemed more out of politeness than real interest in what the Doctor was saying.

"And right across the lake," the Doctor continued, "there's a very different building—the old Feltram house. It's just a ruin now, right at the entrance to the valley. Cloostedd House. It's actually a very scenic spot."

"Right across," the stranger said softly, like he was talking to himself. The Doctor couldn't tell if he was agreeing or asking something.

"That family used to be one of the great ones in this area," the Doctor said. "Now they're completely gone. Hardly anyone even remembers the name."

"Duce ace," mumbled Mr. Hollar, focused on his game.

"While other families have risen even faster," added kind Mr. Peers, who loved talking about family trees and local history.

"Sizes!" shouted the Captain, slamming the table in frustration after a bad roll.

"And there's Snakes Island—another nice view," the Doctor said, trying to keep the conversation going. "They say it got its name from the snakes that used to live there."

"That's not actually true," the stranger said quietly, speaking up for the first time with something of his own. "It should be spelled 'Snaiks.' Old documents call it 'Sen-aiks Island,' named after the seven oak trees that once grew there together."

"Really? That's interesting! I believe it," said the Doctor, now looking at the stranger with curiosity.

"He's right," said Mr. Peers. "Three of those oaks are still there, though two are almost gone. And Clewson of Heckleston has an old document—"

Just then, the landlord came in, a bit out of breath, and walked up to the stranger. "Your carriage is ready, Mr. Feltram. The trunks are loaded, sir."

Mr. Feltram stood up calmly, took out his purse, and asked, "Should I pay at the bar?"

"Whatever you prefer, sir," said Turnbull.

Mr. Feltram gave a polite nod to the men in the room. They smiled, nodded, or waved in return. The Doctor eagerly followed him to the door, happy to welcome him back to Golden Friars. He offered a warm handshake, which Mr. Feltram returned before stepping into the carriage. Once the door closed, the coach rolled quietly away along the moonlit road by the lake, heading toward Mardykes Hall.

After a moment of watching the coach disappear into the night, the men returned to the cozy lounge. The smell of punch still lingered in the air, and Mr. Feltram's untouched tea sat where he had left it. The innkeeper, now back inside, shared what little he knew.

The main thing he said was that Sir Bale was still planning to arrive on the tenth. That was just a few days away. Soon, the excitement would pass, but for now, everyone in Golden Friars was curious and eager to finally meet Sir Bale Mardykes.

Chapter IV.
The Baronet Appears

Just like candles burning blue and the air smelling strange when something evil is near, the peaceful atmosphere of Golden Friars seemed to grow tense and uneasy when people heard that the long-absent Sir Bale Mardykes was returning.

No one ever had anything good to say about him while he was away. In fact, people in the quiet village had heard all kinds of strange and unsettling stories about him. But the farther a story travels, the more details get lost, and it's easier for people to believe that maybe things were misunderstood or blown out of proportion. Even though some good people rolled their eyes and older women frowned at the mention of his name, time had softened people's reactions, and the strange tales were no longer talked about so openly.

Now that Sir Bale was back at Mardykes Hall, many homes in the area held quick discussions. While some judged him harshly right away, most families followed the natural order of things—the powerful draw in the rest—and so the nearby townsfolk made polite visits to the Hall.

Reverend Martin Bedel, the vicar of Golden Friars, was a short, heavyset man with a reddish face, small gray eyes, and a habit of not saying much. He visited the Hall with his talkative wife, who held tightly to his arm.

The drawing-room at Mardykes Hall had a large window in Tudor style that looked out over the lake and the dark purple mountains behind it. Sir Bale wasn't there when they arrived, so Mrs. Bedel used the time to look over the paintings, decorations, and books. She made a few remarks about them, all quite positive, since she wanted to make a good impression. Then she gazed out the window, praising the view.

She was very curious to finally meet Sir Bale, having heard so many dramatic stories about him over the years. She imagined someone like a dark, handsome villain from an old novel—charming and a little dangerous. She was hoping to meet someone full of energy and mystery, a man who knew how to win people over.

She was a bit surprised when he finally showed up.

Sir Bale Mardykes was a middle-aged man, just as she might have remembered if she'd thought about it. He wasn't particularly impressive in appearance. He was average in height, slender, and had dark features. Instead of being lively or charming, he looked serious— even gloomy. The only thing that stood out were his large, dark gray eyes, which were cold and intense.

He moved and spoke like someone who was completely comfortable with himself, but who didn't care much what others thought. It was as if he could be charming if he wanted to, but didn't think it was worth the effort. He gave them each a polite bow—formal enough, but with no smile or warmth.

Still, Sir Bale talked easily. He didn't seem to care what he said or what anyone thought of it. Some of his comments had a sarcastic edge, which Mrs. Bedel, being very literal, didn't always catch.

"I suppose you're the only clergyman around here?" he asked.

"Golden Friars is the closest," said Mrs. Bedel, jumping in to answer for her husband, as she often did. "The next nearest is Wyllarden, and that's thirteen and a half miles away as the bird flies— and more than nineteen by road. Actually, I'd say it's twenty. Ha ha! That's a long way to go for a clergyman."

"Twenty miles by road for thirteen across the air, huh? These road-builders sure know how to make money. They make you take the long way around to enjoy more of the scenery. Only the person paying for the road likes it straight. Everyone else gets dragged along."

"That's very true, Sir Bale. If you're not in a rush, it doesn't matter. That's how Martin sees it—don't we, Martin? But when you're heading home and thinking of tea and the children—well, then a short trip would be nice."

"Nice to have anything in your favor in this place. So, you have children?"

"Quite a few," Mrs. Bedel said proudly, with a knowing smile. "You'd never guess how many."

"I won't try. I'm just surprised you didn't bring them all."

"That's kind of you to say, Sir Bale. But I couldn't bring them all at once. There are—tell him, Martin—ha ha! There are eleven."

"Sounds lively at the vicarage," said Sir Bale politely. Then he added, "Strange how blessings are handed out. You have eleven children, and I haven't got a single one—at least, none that I know of."

"And if you look straight ahead from here," said Mrs. Bedel, "you see the lake, then the mountains, and five miles beyond that you reach Fottrell—which is twenty-five miles by road—"

"Everything is so far apart here! My gardener told me asparagus grows poorly in this area. Seems like clergy do too—no offense," he added, glancing at the vicar, who was rather round.

"Before you came in, we were looking out the window," said Mrs. Bedel. "Your view of the lake and the mountains—it's stunning! You have the best view from this side."

"Truly! I wish I could blast those mountains apart with a shotgun and be done with them. But since I'm stuck with them, I guess I should learn to admire them. We're pretty much married to them now, and arguing won't help."

"I'm sure you don't mean that, Sir Bale," Mrs. Bedel laughed. "You wouldn't change a thing about Mardykes Hall."

"You can't get a breath of air in this place, or even see the sunrise, because of those mountains," he grumbled, frowning at the peaks.

"Well, at least you must like the lake, right?" she asked hopefully.

"No, I don't," he said bluntly. "I'd drain it if I could. It's gloomy. A dark lake surrounded by empty hills—it's awful. I don't know what my ancestors were thinking, building a house right by the water. Maybe they liked the fish. Pike—what a miserable fish! I don't know how people eat it. I wouldn't touch it. I'd sooner eat a guard's spear."

"I thought with all your traveling, Sir Bale, that you'd have grown fond of this kind of landscape," said Mrs. Bedel. "You see a lot of it in Europe, don't you? And there's boating."

"Boating, dear Mrs. Bedel, is the most boring thing in the world. People think because a boat looks nice from shore, the shore must look nice from the boat—but it doesn't. Once you're in the boat, it feels like you've fallen into a hole. You can't see a thing. I hate boats and I hate water. I'd rather have my house near a flat, soggy field—bleak and boring as that is—than be trapped by mountains or drown in a black lake like a kitten. Oh, by the way, there's lunch in the next room. Would you care for some?"

Chapter V.
Mrs. Julaper's Room

Now that Sir Bale Mardykes was settled into his family's old home, people had more time to form their opinions about him. Most didn't like him. His behavior often came off as rude and unpredictable, and sometimes he acted with a kind of cold arrogance. He could be angry and offensive without warning.

The only person he treated consistently was Philip Feltram. Feltram acted like a personal assistant, handling tasks and errands that weren't suitable for regular servants. But in many ways, Sir Bale treated him worse than the staff. He shouted at him, blamed him for everything that went wrong—whether it was in the house, the stables, or out in the fields—and constantly insulted him. People often said he treated Feltram worse than a dog.

Why did Feltram put up with such cruel treatment? What choice did he have? It's the same question people ask when they see soldiers willingly accept harsh punishments. The answer lies in hopelessness. Deep down, people weigh their options—even if they don't realize it—and sometimes decide that staying in a bad situation is still better than risking something worse. Everyone makes these silent choices every day, and they shape how we live, even if no one else sees the struggle behind them.

Most people said, "Any decent man would rather break rocks by the roadside than live like that." But Feltram wasn't sure he'd even be hired to do that kind of work—or that he'd be strong enough to keep the job. He had other thoughts about his future, other plans quietly forming in his mind.

Mrs. Julaper, the warm-hearted old housekeeper at Mardykes Hall, was always kind to Feltram. She was kind to anyone who was hurting. She was one of those people who naturally listen to others' troubles— someone others confide in without fear. And unlike the old story of the reeds whispering secrets to the wind, Mrs. Julaper's secrets stayed safe.

Her room still exists in the oldest part of the house, although the main housekeeper's quarters are now somewhere else. Her cozy room was covered in dark wooden panels up to the ceiling, which was decorated with patterns from the time of King James I. A few faded portraits hung there—paintings that had been removed from more important rooms over time and forgotten. One showed a woman in white satin and a ruffled collar, another a man with a sharp beard and a hawk on his wrist, whose legs had faded from the canvas. Another portrait, barely visible in the shadows, showed a man in a black wig and a steel chest plate with a faint sash across it. That was Sir Guy Mardykes, who had fought with Dundee and died at Killiecrankie. After his death, the more cautious members of the Mardykes family had moved his portrait to this quiet room, where it stayed, out of sight.

At the back of Mrs. Julaper's room was a second door that opened onto a small balcony overlooking the large kitchen. From there, she used to give orders to the cook and oversee the kitchen's work.

On one shelf, she kept her Bible, The Whole Duty of Man, and The Pilgrim's Progress. Next to them were her housekeeping books— some full of handwritten recipes, and others with old-fashioned remedies and treatments once used by generous women of past centuries. A historian today would find them priceless.

Gentle, half-distracted Philip Feltram would often come to her with tears in his eyes, sharing how badly he'd been treated and saying he wished he were dead. And kind Mrs. Julaper, who remembered him as a little boy, would comfort him with a piece of cold pie, a sip of cherry brandy, or a warm cup of coffee—some small treat to lift his spirits.

"Oh, ma'am, I'm tired of this life. What's the point of living if I'm never left in peace, always treated worse than a dog? Wouldn't it be better just to be dead? I think about it all the time. Day and night. I don't care anymore. I think I'll tell him exactly what I think. I can't take it anymore."

"Now, now, don't get yourself so worked up," she said, gently. "Here, drink this. And don't take things so hard. He doesn't mean half of what he says. That's just how people in that family talk sometimes— sharp tongues, but no real harm. You mustn't let words cut so deep. Remember, mean words can't hurt you unless you let them. They don't break bones, do they? I'll make us a nice cup of tea—you like tea—and we'll sit together and enjoy it. Just look at how lovely the sun is on the lake this evening."

She gently patted his shoulder as she stood beside him in her neat dark dress. Her small rosy face smiled down at him. Even as an older woman, she was still quite pretty. Her skin must have been very delicate when she was younger. Even now, her wrinkles were so fine you barely noticed them from a short distance. When she smiled, her cheeks looked as smooth and fresh as two little apples.

"Look out there," she said, nodding toward the deep-set window. "See how bright and peaceful everything looks in the evening light? Isn't that better than any painting in the world? And look how Snakes Island glows."

Feltram raised his eyes and looked sadly out the window.

"That island bothers me, Mrs. Julaper."

"Everything bothers you lately, you silly goose," she said kindly. "If you keep pouting, I'll have to tug your ear." She gave him a playful pinch and laughed.

"I'm going to the still-room now—water's boiling. I'll make us some tea. But if you're still this gloomy when I get back, I'll throw the whole pot out the window, I swear!"

And the view Feltram saw really was beautiful, framed by the old stone window. The closest part of the lake glowed warmly in the golden evening light. The far side lay in shadow under the tall mountains. Against that dark background, Snakes Island stood out sharply—its rocky edges glowing bright yellow in the sun.

But no matter how beautiful the view was, it couldn't calm the sad and anxious man staring at it. For him, even the prettiest part of the scene carried a quiet sense of fear. Left alone, he got up, leaned on the window, and looked out. Then, with a shiver, he squeezed his hands together and started pacing the room, clearly upset.

He didn't notice when Mrs. Julaper quietly came back. She saw him walking around the room like that and thought to herself, as he leaned on the windowsill again:

"It's just plain wrong to worry someone until they're in this state. Sir Bale always had to take things out on someone—man or animal, it didn't matter. He always had to hate something and couldn't let it go. It's a shame, really. Maybe he couldn't help it. Maybe it was just how he was. But still, it was awful to see."

Just then, a maid brought in the tea tray and set it down. Mrs. Julaper gently pulled Philip over by the arm and sat him at the table.

"Now, what good does it do to wear yourself out like that?" she said. "Really, I'm ashamed of you, Master Philip! You take three lumps of sugar, don't you? And lots of cream? Come on now—smile a little!"

"You're always so kind, Mrs. Julaper. You're so cheerful. After I sit with you a while, I start to feel... almost happy," he said, tears starting to fall.

She didn't draw attention to it. She knew him well by now and just kept chatting in her usual cheerful way while she fixed his tea just the way he liked it. He quickly wiped his eyes, hoping she hadn't noticed.

Soon the mood in the room began to lift. Feltram, poor and gentle as he was, loved nothing more than a cup of tea, a cozy conversation, and the company of sweet, talkative Mrs. Julaper. When she spoke of old memories, it brought a little light into his gloomy thoughts, and he felt like those distant childhood days came back to life.

Once he started to feel better, pulled back into those kinder memories by the sound of her voice, he said:

"Sometimes I think I wouldn't mind things so much if I weren't always so nervous and low. Maybe I'm just not feeling well."

"Well, tell me what's bothering you, child," she said, "and I bet I have something on my shelf that'll help."

"It's not something like that," he replied. "Though if I needed medicine, I'd rather have you give it than any doctor."

Mrs. Julaper couldn't help but smile at that. She was proud of her homemade remedies and liked being trusted. Even if Feltram didn't mean to flatter her, his words warmed her heart.

"No, I'm really fine. I haven't felt physically better in ages. It's just... the dreams, ma'am. You wouldn't believe them."

"Well now, dreams can mean different things," she said gently. "Some don't mean anything at all—just noise, like the water lapping the shore. But others mean something. Some are just nonsense, and some are warnings or blessings. Lady Mardykes—God rest her—used to be very good at reading dreams. That was Sir Bale's grandmother, you know. Here, have another cup of tea. And listen to those crows flying over the roof on their way home—what a racket! And see how high they're flying? That means we'll have good weather. So, tell me, what do you dream about? Maybe it's not so bad. Some dreams look scary and feel scary, but they turn out to mean something good in the end."

Chapter VI.
The Intruder

"Well, Mrs. Julaper, I've had dreams like everyone else, young and old," said Mr. Feltram sadly, leaning back in his chair with his hands in his pockets, staring at the floor. "But this one—it's stuck with me, ma'am. I feel like it's taken hold of me. Like something's inside me."

"Inside you, child? What do you mean?"

"I think something's trying to control me. Maybe this is how people go mad. But it won't leave me alone. I've seen it three times—can you believe that?"

"Well now, dear, and what exactly have you seen?" she asked, trying to sound cheerful, even though she was getting a little nervous. The idea of anyone going mad—even gentle Philip—was unsettling.

"Do you remember that full-length portrait, the one without a frame? The lady in the white satin gown? She was beautiful—strangely sad," he added quietly, almost talking to himself. Then, more clearly, he said, "The one in the white gown, with the little lace cap and blue ribbons, holding a bouquet in her hand. You know who she was, right?"

"That was your great-grandmother, my dear," said Mrs. Julaper, lowering her eyes. "It was a real shame what happened to that painting. The boys in the pantry used it as a tray for a whole year—washed glasses on it and everything. It was the prettiest picture in the house. Her face looked so gentle and rosy."

"Well, it's not gentle or rosy anymore," said Philip. "Now it's stiff like a statue, with thin lips and this hard look in her nose. Do you

34

remember that woman they found dead in the valley when I was a boy? The one they said was murdered by gypsies—mean-looking woman?"

"Heavens, Master Philip! Don't go comparing that scary woman to your sweet great-grandmother!"

"Faces can change. That's not what scares me, though—it's the way she talks to me. She's trying to use me for something. It's like she's getting into my thoughts, like she's taking up space in my head. Like she has a say in what I think and do. It's always the same thing, over and over, like a straight beam of light across the lake. That's what she's become now. Oh, God help me!"

"Now stop all that talk," said Mrs. Julaper firmly. "You're just feeling low because Sir Bale's been sharp with you lately. When your spirits get low, you start thinking all kinds of dark things."

"It's not in my head," he said quickly, giving her a wary glance. "But you asked what I dreamed. I don't care if everyone knows. I dreamed I went down a staircase under the lake and got a message. Of course, there aren't any stairs near Snakes Island—we all know that," he added with a hollow laugh. "I know I'm down, like you said... and... oh, Mrs. Julaper, I just wish I was in my coffin, resting."

"Now that's no way to talk, Master Philip. Think about the good things in your life instead of making big problems out of little ones. Sir Bale's short temper isn't worth crying over—not like the way you do. You can't take everything so hard."

"You're probably right, Mrs. Julaper. I know I overreact sometimes," said Philip gently. "I probably let it get to me too much. I'll try to be better. I am his secretary, and I know I'm not the sharpest, so it makes sense that he gets frustrated sometimes. I should be more understanding. It's just... this dream, this worry—it's been eating at me. I'm not myself. And I've let it drag me down. I think it's my fault, really."

"That's a smart way to look at it, my boy. But I'm not saying it's your fault—not at all. We all get upset sometimes, like we get a headache. Only a fool would blame you for that. Sure, the master has his moods—he can be sour and snap at us all if he feels like it. But who doesn't have faults? We have to put up with each other and make the best of things. So come on, cheer up, Philip. Don't you remember that old rhyme I used to tell you when you were little?

'Be always as merry as ever you can,

For no one delights in a sorrowful man.'

So don't go getting up and pacing around the room like that, with your hands in your pockets, staring out the windows and sighing. You look so miserable it breaks my heart. You need to cheer up. Maybe you're just hungry and don't know it. I'll ask the cook to make you something hot."

"But I'm not hungry, Mrs. Julaper. You're too kind. Honestly, I don't deserve it. If it weren't for you, I think I'd have given up long ago."

"And I'll make you a warm drink. How about a glass of punch? Come on now, you have to."

"But I really do prefer the tea, Mrs. Julaper. I mean it," said Philip.

"Tea's no good when your heart's heavy, lad. You need something with a little fire in it—something hot to lift your spirits, get your blood moving, and put a bit of boldness in your talk. How about a bit of something grilled first? No? Well then, you'll have a drop of punch— don't try to argue," she said with a kind smile.

And just like that, Philip gave in to her kindness.

There wasn't a softer soul than Philip Feltram, or a kinder one than Mrs. Julaper, anywhere in the world.

Philip, who barely spoke to anyone else, would often come into her room with tears in his eyes, take her hands in his, and look down at her face sadly as he cried.

"Have you ever heard of anyone like me? Honestly, have you? You know who I am, Mrs. Julaper—you know the truth. People call me Feltram, but Sir Bale knows just as well as I do that's not my real name. I'm Philip Mardykes. Some other man in my place would have fought for his name, his title—just like she keeps whispering in my ear I should do. But you know that wouldn't be right. My grandmother was married—she was the real Lady Mardykes. Imagine seeing someone like her thrown out, and her children stripped of their name. You can't imagine how that feels—not unless you were me. You couldn't know."

"Now, now, Master Philip, don't talk like that," she said gently. "You know Sir Bale wouldn't take kindly to that sort of talk. It's an old story now, and nothing can really be proven. I think—though I can't be sure—that your grandmother might have been tricked. Still, I believe with all my heart she thought she was truly married. Maybe the law found something wrong with it, but I know she was an honorable lady. And what's the use in digging up old pain? How could you prove anything now? The dead don't speak, child. They say dead mice feel no cold—and the dead don't care anymore. So don't stir up trouble. Walls have ears, and you might say something you can't take back. And remember—when you can't win a fight, don't start one."

"Fight him? Oh, Mrs. Julaper! You don't really think I'd do that?" Philip cried, shocked. "You don't know me if you think I'd hurt Sir Bale. That never crossed my mind—not for a second. I'm just upset. I complain too much because I'm so miserable. But please, believe me—I never meant to go after him in court or anything like that! I just want to clear my family's name. That's all. I don't care about his money—don't you know that about me? I'd never attack the man who's been feeding me all these years. I'd hate myself if I ever did. Please, Mrs. Julaper, say you don't believe I would!"

The poor man broke down in tears, and kind Mrs. Julaper comforted him with her soft voice.

"Thank you, ma'am. Thank you. I swear I'd never hurt Bale or even worry him if I could help it. It's just that I'm—so unhappy. I keep thinking of what to do and where to go next. Just a small thing could push me to leave Mardykes. I'll go—not in anger, Mrs. Julaper, please don't think that. But I can't stay. I've got to leave."

"Now, now," she said gently, "there's no reason to talk like that. Nothing's happened that should upset you this badly. Sure, Sir Bale can be short-tempered and harsh sometimes, but I know he cares about you. If he didn't, he would've told me long ago. He likes you more than you think."

Suddenly a loud voice rang out in the hallway.

"Hullo! I say, where the devil is Mr. Feltram?" Sir Bale shouted, his voice sharp and angry.

"Oh no—it's him," whispered Mrs. Julaper. "You'd better go."

"D—n it! Does no one hear me? Mrs. Julaper! Hello? Anyone home? D—n it all, will nobody answer me?" Sir Bale's voice roared through the hall as he began banging on the wall with his walking stick, making a loud, rattling noise.

Mrs. Julaper, now a little pale, opened her door and stood in the doorway with her hand on the knob. She gave a quick curtsy as Sir Bale marched toward her. His face was furious, and he stamped his foot.

"Well, ma'am, I'm glad to see you at least! Can you tell me where Feltram is?"

"He's in my room, Sir Bale. Should I tell him you're looking for him?"

"No need, thank you," the baronet growled. "I've got a voice, haven't I?" He stormed down the hall toward the housekeeper's room, gripping his cane tightly, eyes burning, and jaw clenched like a man about to strike a horse that had just pushed him too far.

Chapter VII.
The Bank Note

Sir Bale pushed past Mrs. Julaper as he stormed into her room, where he found Philip Feltram waiting quietly, though he looked tired and sad, not scared.

If anyone had seen Sir Bale just then, they might have expected violence—his face was pale, his eyes angry, and he was gripping his cane so tightly it shook. But he had no intention of hitting anyone. Even so, he was clearly furious. He stopped a few steps from Feltram and glared at him, his voice sharp.

"I've been looking for you, Mr. Feltram. I need a word—if you're finished with your little tea party," he said, motioning sharply toward the tea tray with the end of his cane. "Come with me. Five minutes in the library."

Sir Bale stared at him coldly, clearly suspicious, as if he expected Feltram to look guilty. Then he turned and walked quickly toward the library, not waiting for a reply. Feltram followed, and by the time he got there, Sir Bale was already standing on the hearthrug, his back to the fire, heels together, cane in hand like a soldier waiting for inspection.

Feltram stepped into the room but stopped just inside the doorway, feeling nervous under the baronet's hard stare. He didn't walk any farther in.

"Close the door," said Sir Bale. "That's good. Come closer. I don't want to shout what I'm about to say."

He cleared his throat and kept his eyes locked on Feltram.

"Just a few days ago, you said you wished you had a hundred pounds. Am I right?"

"Yes, I believe so."

"You believe so? Don't play dumb—you know you did. You said you wanted to leave. And I had no issue with that—especially now. Are you following me?"

"Yes, Sir Bale. I understand."

"I bet you do," said Sir Bale, sneering. "Here's something strange. You want a hundred pounds. You can't earn it. You can't borrow it. But it just so happens that I had a £100 banknote locked in that desk over there." He jabbed his cane at it angrily. "That's where I kept it, along with the papers you work on. There are only two keys—one with me, one with you. No one else has one. So, you starting to get the picture? Don't bother lying."

Feltram was beginning to understand—Sir Bale thought he had stolen the money. But he didn't know exactly how to respond, and he looked very shaken.

"Hah! I thought you'd start to get it," Sir Bale snapped. "It's not fun explaining something to someone who already knows the story. But I'll keep it short. I go to the desk to get the note so I can pay the crown dues—you know about those—and when I open the drawer, guess what? It's gone. The note is gone!"

He paused, watching Feltram closely. Feltram swallowed hard and tried to speak, but no words came out.

"It's gone. And we both know where it went. I didn't take it. You're the only other one with access. You said you wanted to leave—and I won't stop you—but you're not leaving with that money. Hand it over now, or deal with the consequences."

"Oh, God," Feltram said, shaking. "I feel so sick."

"Of course you do. Anyone would feel sick after swallowing a banknote. It's hard to give it up—like pulling a tooth. But don't think I'm stupid. Just hand it over quietly."

"I swear to God—"

"Yeah, and may He strike you down if you're lying. Because if you don't give it up, I'll go to the magistrate, get a warrant, and have everything searched—your pockets, your bags, the whole lot."

Feltram blinked, stunned. "Is this really happening?" he muttered.

"It sure is. You're not dreaming, and neither am I," said Sir Bale. "Do you have the note on you?"

"No! God forbid! Sir—Sir Bale—please. Bale, you can't really believe I'd do this! You've known me since I was a little boy—when I wasn't even as tall as this table—and—"

He burst into tears.

"Cut the waterworks," Sir Bale growled. "Just give me the note. You know I need it. And I swear I'll make things worse for you if you force me to. I've said what I needed to say."

He motioned to the door. Feltram, pale as a ghost and shaken to the core, left the room in a daze. He didn't even realize where he was walking until he found himself outside Mrs. Julaper's door. He pressed his hand hard against his chest, and the first breath he noticed was a shaky sob. He looked out the window but didn't see a thing. His mind was spinning.

Nothing in his life had ever hurt him this deeply. This was the moment he truly understood how much pain he could feel without losing his mind—and how much it took to stay standing when your heart felt broken and your thoughts were crashing into each other like waves in a storm.

Meanwhile, Sir Bale left the room as well, still angry, though not quite as sure about things as he had been. He believed Feltram took the money—but there had been something strange in his reaction. Some of it made the baronet more certain, but other parts gave him pause.

Sir Bale walked to the edge of the lake, just where the shadow of the house reached the shore. He looked out toward Snakes Island.

There were two things about Mardykes that he truly hated.

One was Philip Feltram. Right or wrong, he had the nagging feeling that Feltram knew more about his past than was safe.

The other was the lake. It was a beautiful lake—he could admit that. He had enough taste in art to recognize a perfect scene. And while he was a strong rower and enjoyed other lakes, something about this one filled him with dread. The feeling came from years of strange thoughts, bad dreams, and memories he never spoke about.

Even people who laugh off religion often end up haunted by superstition. Sir Bale's fear of the lake came from deep inside—built from bad signs, strange feelings, and thoughts he didn't want to admit. But they stayed with him anyway.

He stood with one foot resting on the side of a boat, chained to the shore. But he wouldn't step into it—not for anything. Something told him that lake held danger. He didn't know what or how or when, but he felt sure that one day, it would destroy him.

He stared out at the calm water, toward the rocky little island in the distance, thinking about Philip Feltram. The setting sun lit up his face, casting golden light across his sharp, brooding features and leaving his deep-set eyes in shadow. His expression resembled the cold, distant look of Charles II in old portraits.

Who among us really lives in the moment, like children do? Who doesn't chase happiness far off in the distance, as Sidney Smith said— like a man searching for his hat when it's already on his head?

Sir Bale, trapped in his bitterness toward both Feltram and the lake, stood lost in his dark thoughts. It would've done him good to stop listening to that imaginary raven croaking bad news in his ear, and instead enjoy the peaceful sounds of the birds all around, singing in the warm golden light of the sunset.

Chapter VIII.
Feltram's Plan

Sir Bale's deep fear of the beautiful lake—which others thought was stunning—was rooted in pure superstition, even though he pretended not to believe in such things. As a child, he'd been frightened by old stories about Snakes Island, and those tales had stuck with him, whether he admitted it or not. He had strange dreams he never spoke about. A fortune-teller in Germany once told him that his worst enemy would come from a lake. Someone else in France had said something similar. And one time, while waiting alone in a hotel room in Lucerne before heading out on the lake, something odd happened. A sunburned man with a thin, wicked-looking face suddenly appeared at his open window. The man leaned on the frame, stuck his head into the room, and said in a rough accent, "Waiting, are you? You'll get enough of the lake one day. Don't worry—they'll come for you when the time's right." Then he smirked cruelly and walked away.

It was so sudden, and so in line with the thoughts Bale had just been having about the lake back home, that it shook him. He laughed it off and looked outside, thinking of offering the man money to explain what he meant, but the man had vanished.

If Bale hadn't already been obsessed with omens and fears tied to the lake, he might not have even remembered the incident. But because he was, he couldn't forget it. He was ashamed of his fear but couldn't get rid of it. The roots of it all went back to his childhood, to ghost stories told by the fire that had sunk into his imagination.

There's a large bedroom in Mardykes Hall said to have belonged to the woman who tragically drowned in the lake. Mrs. Julaper was sure of it. Her aunt, who had lived to be very old, remembered the woman's death and heard stories about it from even older folks who knew everything about the Feltram family and Mardykes back then.

That bedroom had a view of Snakes Island, the mountains, and the lake. It was a grand but gloomy room, filled with old-fashioned furniture. People said it was haunted, especially when the wind came from the direction of Golden Friars—the same direction as the night she died—or when storms rolled over the mountains and lightning flashed across the water.

One night, long after the tragedy, a lady guest who knew nothing about the room's past stayed there. She loved dramatic weather, so she asked her maid to leave the shutters open so she could watch the storm. As it approached, she fell asleep.

She woke later to the loud roar of thunder, just as the storm reached the lake. As she watched the sky flash, she saw a woman at the window. Her hair and dress were soaking wet, and she looked terrified as she shook the window violently. Before the lady could react, the woman wrung her hands, threw herself backward, and disappeared.

The guest assumed she had seen someone caught in the storm, unable to get in, who had then gone to another door. She went back to sleep. It wasn't until morning, when she looked out the window, that she remembered—her room was thirty feet above the ground.

There was another story, too. Mr. Randal Rymer, a preacher who had once been a soldier, visited Mardykes often. He had a habit of sleeping with his window open, no matter the weather. One night, as he lay in bed with the moonlight shining in, he saw a pale figure slip through the window and move toward the fireplace, where a few embers still glowed. The figure crouched over it, stretching out its hands for warmth. When Mr. Rymer moved in bed, the figure turned to him. Its eyes, huge and pale, looked like melting snow in the moonlight. Then it raised its arms toward the chimney and seemed to dissolve into the smoke and vanish.

Sir Bale didn't like Feltram. His father, Sir William, had left a letter that supposedly set up money for Philip Feltram. It was found with the will, and addressed to Bale.

"That belongs to me," Sir Bale had said, slipping the letter into his pocket. No one ever saw it again.

But Mr. Charles Twyne, the local lawyer, used to say—especially when drunk—that he knew something about that letter. According to him, it gave Philip two hundred pounds a year, to be paid from the Harfax estate. It wasn't a legal order, but a clear instruction. Sir Bale was supposed to be the trustee. But after hiding the letter, he'd been keeping that money for himself.

Twyne was careful about who he talked to. He was afraid of Sir Bale and hated that he had chosen a different lawyer from a nearby town. So people weren't sure if Twyne was telling the truth or just rambling. The one thing that made his story believable was how obviously Sir Bale disliked Feltram. Why else would he keep someone he hated so close? It seemed like he was forced to tolerate him, maybe out of guilt.

Then came the fight over the missing banknote. Sir Bale had his doubts—part of him wasn't sure Feltram had taken it. Philip's behavior looked honest. But the situation still looked suspicious. And Sir Bale was quick to assume the worst, valuing proof and logic more than trust or character. Even when he felt uncertain, he never let Feltram know.

For two days, Sir Bale didn't say a word to him. He walked past him in the halls without a glance, brooding and planning what to do next.

Feltram, during those two days, was filled with dread. He wanted to leave, but doing so now would seem like an admission of guilt. Somewhere deep down, he still hoped that fate—or justice—would clear his name.

Mrs. Julaper tried her best to comfort him. She trusted him completely and was furious at the accusations. Her heart broke for him, and she cried with him. But Sir Bale never softened. Maybe he was secretly glad to finally have an excuse to get rid of Feltram—someone who might know too much about his past.

Then came another cold meeting. Sir Bale told Feltram that unless the note was returned by ten the next morning, he had to leave.

Feltram had already decided to leave. But where would he go? He didn't really care, as long as he could find some way to survive.

He thought about an old couple who lived across the lake, on land that once belonged to the Feltrams. They lived high up on the hills, where trees grew thin. They had sheep, goats, and lived quietly. They were fond of Philip, maybe out of loyalty to his family. Philip had grown up in that tough landscape. Cold and rain didn't bother him. And they might be happy to have his help with the farm.

This was the only plan he had.

So, when he visited Mrs. Julaper and told her he was going to leave that night—cross the lake in Tom Marlin's boat and hike up the hill to the old farm—she was horrified.

"You're not going anywhere tonight!" she cried. "You'll come sit in the little room here where he can't follow you. We'll talk this through.

This isn't a night for wandering off. It would take over an hour just to cross the lake, and even longer to get up the hill. If night catches you on the mountain, you could lose your life. There's a storm coming—they've heard thunder rolling in from Blarwyn Fells. No one should be out tonight, least of all you."

Chapter IX.
The Crazy Parson

Mrs. Julaper had lived so long among the wild hills and valleys that she'd grown good at reading the signs of the weather. In a place like Golden Friars, where there isn't much else to watch, people learn to read nature's warnings—how the clouds gather around certain cliffs, how the lake changes color, or how mist clings to a mountain. She had a feeling a storm was coming—and she was right.

The sun had set more than an hour ago, and the sky had gone completely dark. A huge thunderstorm, which had been rumbling faintly beyond the mountains all afternoon like an army marching in the distance, was now right overhead. It roared over the rocky valleys on the far side of the lake and lit up the surface of the water like polished steel whenever lightning struck. Fierce winds howled down the hills, whipping the trees, tearing off their dry leaves, and sending them flying through the air. If you looked out the window, you'd see little between lightning flashes—but each time the sky lit up, it showed the trees thrashing, waves crashing, and foam churning on the lake.

In the middle of all this chaos, someone suddenly began pounding on the front door of Mardykes Hall. It's hard to say how long they'd been knocking before a lull in the storm made it loud enough to hear.

Sir Bale Mardykes didn't hire fancy servants, but he had enough of them. One of them, the son of an old tenant, opened the door. The wind and rain were mostly on the far side of the house, so the front was partly sheltered. Standing there in the wind was a thin old man, muttering what might have been a prayer. His long silver hair was soaked and blowing in the wind. His sharp, intense features and wide, wandering eyes made him look wild. He wore a worn-out black coat, high leather gaiters buckled above his knees, and a strange wide hat with a handkerchief tied over it to keep it from blowing off.

The servant knew who he was right away and greeted him with a mix of respect and fear. He invited the man inside and offered him a seat by the fire.

"Go to your master," said the old man in a rough voice, "and tell him I have a message from someone he hasn't seen in forty-two years."

While he spoke, he untied the handkerchief from his hat and shook the water off it.

The servant went to the library, where Sir Bale sat by the fire.

"What is it?" barked Sir Bale, turning sharply with an annoyed look.

"It's 't sir comin', Sir Bale," the servant replied, using the northern way of referring to a clergyman as "sir."

"What sir?"

"Sir Hugh Creswell, if you please, Sir Bale."

"Oh! Mad Creswell? That crazy preacher?" said Sir Bale. "Tell Mrs. Julaper to give him some food and find him a bed. That's what he wants. These crazy people know where to find shelter."

But before the servant could leave, the loud voice of the old preacher rang out behind him.

"No, Sir Bale Mardykes, that is not what I want," he said, stepping into the room. "Mardykes Hall has always welcomed me in the past, and I thank the house for it. But tonight, I'll be moving on to Pindar's Bield, three miles up the lake. That's where I'll rest."

"Why not stay here, Mr. Creswell?" asked Sir Bale. Even though he thought the man was crazy, people had a strange respect for him. He was seen as a holy wanderer, and there was a kind of fear about offending him. No one knew where he came from or where he went. Once a year or so, he would appear at a farm deep in the hills, stay one night, and disappear the next morning. He lived a hard life, was deeply religious, and was a bit strange—which made people both respect and fear him.

"I won't sleep at Mardykes tonight," said the old man. "I won't eat, drink, or sit down—not even warm my hands by your fire. I come like the man of God from Judah, sent to King Jeroboam. I'm here with a warning. And like that prophet, I say, 'Even if you gave me half your house, I would not go in or eat or drink with you.'"

"Suit yourself," said Sir Bale, a little annoyed. "Say what you came to say. You're welcome to stay or go—though you'd be mad to travel on a night like this."

"Leave us," said the preacher, waving the servant away. "What I have to say is for your master only."

Sir Bale nodded, and the servant left, closing the door behind him.

The old man stepped closer to Sir Bale and lowered his voice just a little. He paused whenever the thunder crashed nearby.

"Tell me, Sir Bale—what's going on between you and Philip Feltram?"

Surprised by the question, Sir Bale told him, in a short and cold way, what had happened.

"And you're certain of these facts?" asked the old preacher. "You wouldn't accuse your own cousin and old friend of being a thief unless you were completely sure?"

"I am sure," said Sir Bale harshly.

"Then open that cabinet," said the old man, pointing.

"I don't mind," said Sir Bale, and he walked to a tall oak cabinet carved with strange gothic faces and figures. He opened it, revealing rows of small drawers and compartments inside.

"Open the drawer with the red seal on it," Hugh Creswell said, pointing with his thin finger.

Sir Bale did as he was told—and to his shock, there was the missing banknote. As soon as he saw it, a memory hit him. He now clearly remembered putting the note there himself.

"That's the one," Creswell said with a pale smile, locking eyes with Sir Bale. But his smile quickly faded into a stern look. "Last night, I slept near Haworth Moss," he said, "and in a dream, your father came to me. He said, 'My son Bale is blaming Philip for taking a note from his desk. But he forgot—he put it in the cabinet himself. Come with me.' Then, in spirit, I was here in this room. He opened the cabinet and showed me this drawer. There was the note. He told me, 'Go and tell my son to ask Philip Feltram for forgiveness, or he will leave in weakness and return in power.' He said more, but I'm not allowed to repeat it. That's the message. Now let me say something of my own."

He looked hard at Sir Bale, his voice sharp.

"The dead spoke through me, and their words reached you during thunder and lightning. Why have you been so cruel to Philip Feltram? You were so sure you were right—but you were wrong. He's not a fool or a liar. Ask for his forgiveness. You must change, or he will return stronger than before. Remember that. Those words will echo through hills, valleys, and beyond—and they'll change you."

With that, the old man turned, left the room, and walked back into the storm, heading toward Pindar's Bield.

"Well, I'll be..." muttered Sir Bale, still stunned. "That old man barged in here to lecture me—in my own house!" He cursed under his breath. "I don't care what he says—he's not staying here tonight."

He stormed out into the hall and shouted at the servants.

"Get that crazy old man out of here! I don't care how—just make sure he never comes back!"

But Creswell was already gone. He had said what he came to say and meant every word.

Sir Bale slammed the door shut behind him, as if slamming it in Creswell's face.

"Apologize to Feltram? What a joke! Anyone would've believed he was guilty with half the evidence. And I was ready to let him walk away—with my hundred-pound note! Forgive him? Not a chance."

Still, doubt started to sneak in. Deep down, he knew he owed Feltram an apology—or at least an explanation. But he didn't want to admit it. He still disliked him. Feltram was weak, and worse, he knew too much—too much about Sir Bale's dark past in other countries. Feltram had even gently warned him a few times. That only made it worse. Just knowing that Feltram had those secrets felt like an insult. Sir Bale couldn't forgive that. He wished Feltram would disappear. Honestly, if the note hadn't turned up, he would've been fine leaving the situation unresolved.

Outside, the thunder and lightning were still crashing louder than ever. Sir Bale opened the shutter and looked out at the wild storm. For a few moments, he stood there, lost in the dramatic sight.

When he turned back, he noticed the £100 note still in his hand. He gave a dry, bitter smile.

He realized he couldn't let things stay like this. But what should he do? He decided to send for Mrs. Julaper and tell her, casually, that Feltram could stay after all. That should be enough. She could pass on the message.

He called for her. Soon, he heard the jingle of her keys and the light sound of her footsteps in the hallway.

"Mrs. Julaper," he said in a calm voice, "Feltram can stay. You've convinced me. But—why have you been crying?"

Her face, usually cheerful, looked tired and red-eyed. She'd clearly been crying.

"It's too late, sir. He's already gone."

"Gone? When?"

"About half an hour ago, sir. I'm really sorry. It was heartbreaking to see him leave the place where he grew up—especially on a night like this."

"No one told him to leave tonight. Where did he go?"

"I don't know, sir. He left my room while I was upstairs. Janet said she saw him walking past the window not ten minutes after Mr. Creswell left."

"Well then," Sir Bale said, turning away, "there's no point thinking more about it. He made his decision. And since that's what he wanted—so be it. Good night."

Chapter X.
Adventure in Tom Marlin's Boat

Philip Feltram used to be well liked. He was gentle, kind, and a little shy. Before he became so sad and broken, he enjoyed jokes and funny stories, and he used to laugh easily. Now that he was gone, who would Sir Bale pick on? Who would take the blame for everything without a fight?

Sir Bale started to feel something close to guilt. The more he thought about Hugh Creswell's strange visit and warning, the more uneasy he felt. The storm outside still roared, and even Sir Bale had to admit it was harsh that Feltram left on such a terrible night. Yes, he had left on his own—but would people really believe that? And would he have left at all if Sir Bale had just done what Creswell suggested—spoken kindly to him, explained about the banknote, and maybe apologized? Feltram had left only a few minutes after Creswell. If Sir Bale had acted just a little sooner, maybe none of this would've happened. But now it was too late. Sir Bale decided to let things play out on their own.

While standing by the window, lost in thought, he heard voices outside mixing with the storm. He looked out and saw three men moving through the darkness, carrying something heavy. They passed under the window and around the side of the house. In the brief quiet between the thunder, he could hear them talking.

Something about the scene gave him a deep, unexplainable feeling of dread. It reminded him of a dream where you just know something bad is about to happen. He waited, hoping they would come back, but they didn't. The feeling in his chest only grew heavier.

"If they're coming to bother me, they'll find me. They always do," he muttered, trying to shake it off.

He went back to writing the letters he'd been putting off. Feltram usually handled those chores, but since Sir Bale had pushed him away, the work piled up. Still, he couldn't focus. He kept looking at the door, expecting footsteps or a knock.

Finally, he heard Mrs. Julaper's keys jingling and her hurried steps. A moment later, there was a knock on the door—and just as thunder boomed overhead, she burst in, clearly upset.

"Oh, Sir Bale! Oh dear! Philip Feltram's come back—he's dead!"

Sir Bale stared at her.

"Slow down," he said. "Tell me exactly what's happened."

"He's lying on the couch in the old still-room. It's awful. He's drowned. Tom Warren just ran off to Golden Friars to fetch Doctor Torvey."

"Drowned?" Sir Bale repeated. "Or is he just soaked? Show me. I'll see for myself."

With a serious face, Sir Bale followed Mrs. Julaper through the halls. In the still-room, all the house servants were gathered, along with three men from the lake. One of them was soaking wet, with water still dripping from his clothes and hair.

When Sir Bale entered, everyone stepped back. He walked quickly over to where Philip was lying on a low bed by the wall, lit by a few scattered candles. He placed a hand on Feltram's cold, wet chest.

Sir Bale knew what needed to be done. Everyone jumped into action. They took off Feltram's wet clothes, wrapped him in warm blankets, used heating pans and bricks, and tilted his body to help the water drain. They tried to help him breathe with bellows, but nothing worked.

Philip's face remained pale and still. He was cold, silent, and unresponsive, even with all the warmth and effort around him.

Finally, Sir Bale quietly placed a hand on Philip's chest one last time. After a moment, he shook his head.

"He's gone. Yes... poor fellow. He's dead."

Then he turned to the others and said, "Let me be clear: Mrs. Julaper knows I didn't tell him to leave tonight. It was his decision— stubborn and foolish as it was. Maybe he wanted people to think we threw him out, but that's just not true. He was welcome to stay, and Mrs. Julaper can tell you that. Right, Mrs. Julaper?"

"No, sir," she said through her tears.

"Not a single person knew. It was just something he decided to do. And now this is the result. We did everything we could. I don't think even the doctor could've saved him. But does anyone know exactly what happened?"

Two of the men did—one of them being the wet man who had helped carry Feltram back.

Tom Marlin, who lived by the lake in a small stone building that might've once been part of the old Mardykes Castle, began to explain. Tom fished in the lake and rowed people across it for extra money. With his long gray hair and thick eyebrows, he had a rough look and spoke in a strong local accent.

"He came to me this morning," Tom said, "said he'd want the boat to cross the lake. Didn't say when. With the storm coming, I didn't think he'd show up. But just as my wife lit a lamp, he came knocking like mad. Poor lad. He's been looking rough lately, though always kind and gentle."

"He begged me to take him across to the Clough of Cloostedd. My wife said no. I said, 'No way I'm rowing in this storm.' But he kept begging, crying—like he wasn't in his right mind. So I gave in. I figured I'd row near Snakes Island where the wind wasn't as bad, and maybe he'd see for himself how rough the lake was and call it off."

"So off we went—me, Bill, and Philip. We kept the island between us and the wind, but when we passed a certain point, he suddenly stood up and started talking strange. I thought he saw something, but there was nothing there."

"Then I saw something white rise from the water—looked like a hand. Philip leaned over, reached for it, and fell in. I dove in three times before I found him and pulled him back by the hair. But it was too late."

Just as Tom finished his story, the loud ring of the hall bell and a knock at the front door told them someone else had just arrived.

Chapter XI.
Sir Bale's Dream

Doctor Torvey stepped into the old still-room, bundled up in a thick coat and a colorful scarf wrapped partly around his face.

"Well now—what's this? Poor Feltram's had an accident?" he said, speaking to Sir Bale as he walked over to the bed and pulled off his gloves.

"I see you've kept him warm. That's good. And I see a lot of water's come out of his mouth—tilt him a little more that way. Hmm... oh dear." He placed his hand on Feltram and gently moved his limbs. "It's been more than an hour since this happened, hasn't it? I'm afraid there's not much to be done now." He lowered his voice and leaned toward Sir Bale. "You can see the stiffness in his body. It's very sad, but it's over. He's gone. No point trying anything more."

Then, calling over Mrs. Julaper, he asked, "Have you ever seen someone dead before? Look at his eyes, look at his mouth. That should've told you right away." And then again, quietly to Sir Bale, "It's useless now to try anything else."

The Doctor listened to Sir Bale's account of what had happened and nodded along, saying things like, "Exactly right," and "Well done—good thinking."

When he'd finished examining Philip and the people around the bed had gone quiet again, Doctor Torvey stood beside the body with one hand resting on the blanket. "Everyone did everything just right here—exactly what any experienced doctor would have done. I don't believe anything important was missed. If I'd been here from the start, I'm not sure I could've added anything helpful. See here?" He lifted and released Feltram's fingers, which were stiff and frozen in place. "That's how you know he was already gone by the time he got here. So don't worry—there wasn't any delay that cost him his life."

Then, turning to Sir Bale, he said, "If you have any messages for Golden Friars, I'd be happy to carry them."

"No, thank you," said Sir Bale. "It's a sad ending, poor fellow. Let's talk a little more in the study. You'll have a glass of sherry or port—people say the port's not bad here. I don't drink it myself, but still. Mrs. Julaper, please take care of things here, and make sure Marlin and the others get supper and something warm to drink. Marlin, you've been in wet clothes long enough."

With kind words all around, Sir Bale took the Doctor to his study. There, he poured drinks and talked in a friendly way, telling his own version of everything that had happened between him and Feltram. He made himself sound good, and the Doctor—already impressed by the port and the attention—listened and nodded. Sir Bale knew he couldn't afford to lose anyone's support, especially not someone like the Doctor, who visited just about every house in the area at least a few times a year.

By the time the Doctor left to return to Golden Friars, he was in great spirits. He thought highly of Sir Bale, even more highly of the wine, and best of all, of himself. He joked cheerfully into the wind, treating the thunder and lightning like a big fireworks show. If the George and Dragon tavern had still been open, he'd have stopped in right away to share the news and praise Sir Bale as a decent man—and Feltram, unfortunately, as a bit of a fool.

But the tavern was closed. Its windows were dark, and the lightning lit up only the outside. So he went home instead, ready to tell his wife the full story.

Back at Mardykes, Sir Bale's uneasy feelings weren't so much about guilt as they were about keeping his reputation clean. He wasn't sorry Feltram was gone. Feltram had known too much—things that could cause problems if he ever spoke out. Now he wouldn't. The "plug of clay," as Sir Bale thought of it, had silenced him forever. But Sir Bale didn't want people to blame him. Feltram had been popular, and his death stirred up strong emotions. Sir Bale didn't want to be seen as the one who'd driven him away.

His nerves had settled a bit now. It was late, and after writing many letters, he was tired. He pulled his chair closer to the fire, and before long, he dozed off.

The storm was starting to pass. Thunder rolled far off in the mountains, and the wild wind had settled into a quieter, softer sound that almost rocked the world to sleep.

Sir Bale's nap came easily. But his head hung at an awkward angle, which may have led to the strange dream that followed.

It was one of those dreams that seem to begin exactly where waking life leaves off. He dreamed he was still in his chair, in the same room, holding a candle. He got up and walked through the halls to the still-room where Feltram's body lay. The house was silent. He could faintly hear crickets and the ticking of a clock echoing down the corridor.

When he opened the still-room door, the only light was from his candle. Everything looked just as he'd left it. Feltram's face—gentle, now fixed in death—was turned upward, pale and full of pain. Sir Bale looked down at it, feeling unsettled, and pulled the blanket over it.

"Gone in weakness," he muttered, repeating Hugh Creswell's words.

Then a soft voice near him whispered with a deep sigh, "Come in power."

He spun around, but no one was there. The light grew dim, and a heavy dread filled him—especially when he noticed the shape under the blanket beginning to move. Frozen in fear, he backed toward the door, unable to look away.

Then something dark—like a huge black ape—crawled out from the foot of the bed. It leapt at him and grabbed him by the throat. He couldn't breathe. Voices screamed, cursed, and laughed all around him. In the middle of that terror, he woke up.

But was he still dreaming?

Because in the silence that followed, he heard something strange— shrieks echoing down the halls. Were they echoes of his dream, or real cries carried through the house?

Soon, you'll find out exactly what caused the noise.

Chapter XII.
Marcella Bligh and Judith Wale Keep Watch

After sharing some wine with Sir Bale, Doctor Torvey returned to the still-room where Philip Feltram's body had been laid.

Mrs. Julaper had stopped crying and was busy with her usual tasks. Two old women had taken charge of the night watch. They had already cleaned and prepared the body, laying it out neatly in the small bed where Philip had been placed while there was still hope he might recover. The two women were thin, wrinkled, and rather creepy-looking.

Marcella Bligh, who had only one good eye and a sharp nose like a bird's beak, leaned over Philip's face, carefully placing coins on his eyelids to keep them shut. Her blank eye glinted strangely.

Judith Wale, hunched over and pale with twitchy, beady eyes, was moving a bucket of hot water. She wore huge, patched shoes that clattered with every step.

Doctor Torvey knew both women well—they were often called to help when someone had died.

"How are we tonight, Mrs. Bligh?" he said, half-joking. "And Judy—aren't you far from town? Helping poor Mr. Feltram get ready for his last journey, I see. You've done this often, haven't you? Standing guard over the dead like soldiers in a sentry box."

The Doctor stood at the end of the bed, smelling strongly of port wine, hands in his pockets, cheerful and a bit thick-tongued from drink.

Mrs. Julaper would've liked to send him away, but he wasn't cruel—just too comfortable with death.

"You'll need to keep the bandage on tight," he told the women. "You should know by now, if you act fast, the mouth closes easily. Mrs. Julaper, I suppose you'll send for Jos Fringer? Best undertaker in town, I say."

"That depends on what Sir Bale wants," Mrs. Julaper answered quietly.

"You've done a neat job laying him out. Not bad. If you'd waited any longer, it would've been hard to get him into a coffin—he'll need a long one too," the Doctor added. "Life's short, eh? Such a shame. This'll make a stir in town, that's for sure. After all the thunder and drama… I think I'll take a little brandy, Mrs. Julaper, if you don't mind."

The Doctor settled into a chair by the fire, and Mrs. Julaper, though unsure if it was proper, poured him a small glass of brandy. He drank it with a smile, then dozed off by the fire, snoring away like he was at home—not beside a dead man.

Eventually, he woke with a sudden jerk, asked for his scarf and his horse, and took his leave, saying goodbye to the two old women who were still shuffling around the body, whispering and nodding. He also gave a long, professional glance at Philip's body before he left. Mrs. Julaper, relieved, watched him go.

With the doctor gone and everything ready, the house fell quiet. The storm was finally dying down. The thunder now rumbled far away, and the wild wind had turned into a sad, slow moan. Inside the house, everything was still. The two old women, each hardened by life and used to death, settled in by the fire, oddly comfortable in each other's company. They made tea, chatted about their aches and pains, and shared memories of past wakes and odd stories of the dead.

They spoke of bodies that grew taller in coffins, of people buried alive, and of ghosts that walked after death.

"Have you ever been down by Haworth, near Dalworth Moss?" Mrs. Wale asked, spoon in hand.

"No, not that far south," replied Mrs. Bligh. "But my father used to cut peat there."

"Did you know Farmer Dykes, who lived by Lin-tree Scaur?" Wale asked. "I laid him out myself. He could be cruel, but he always made sure I ate well when I visited. A year after he died, Tom Ettles was walking near Birken Stoop and saw a strange white ball rolling down the road. It led him to a gravel pit, and there, stuck with his horse, was Farmer Dykes—dead as anything, but right in front of him. The horse was Black Captain—shot years before the farmer even died! Dykes begged Tom to help him out, but Tom refused. The ghost threatened him, and Tom ran home, scared out of his wits."

Their heads had drawn close together during the tale, and their voices dropped to a hushed murmur—when suddenly, they heard a strange, low laugh coming from near the door.

Both turned in shock—and saw Philip Feltram sitting straight up in bed. He held the white bandage in one hand, and one foot hung off the bed, as if he were about to get up.

Mrs. Bligh screamed and grabbed Mrs. Wale, who shrieked and clung back. They both forgot all politeness, stumbling and tugging at each other to get away—each trying to hide behind the other as they screamed louder than ever before.

These were the cries that had torn through the house and woken Sir Bale from his nightmare—now loud enough to wake everyone else too.

Chapter XIII.
The Mist on the Mountain

Early the next morning, Doctor Torvey was called back, full of questions, disbelief, and scientific curiosity. But once he saw Philip Feltram alive and recovering, he couldn't deny what was right in front of him.

"Honestly, Sir Bale, I wouldn't have believed it if I hadn't seen it with my own eyes," the Doctor said, sipping sherry in the breakfast parlor, a large room with wooden panels and paintings. "No pulse—none! No breath at all—he was as cold as one of those garden statues. You might say those signs could be wrong, but what about the stiffness? Old Judy Wale and her friend Marcella, or 'Monocula' if you like, they both saw it. They know the signs of death as well as I do—maybe better. They'll swear to it. I'm going to write this whole case up and send it to my old mentor, Sir Hervey Hansard, in London. The medical world is going to be shocked. Nothing like this has ever happened—and I doubt it ever will again."

While the Doctor went on and on, Sir Bale sat back in his chair, arms crossed and legs stretched out. He stared up at a portrait of a tall woman in a white satin dress, with a bird on her hand, painted with an arrogant smile. He didn't look very impressed.

"You doctors are definitely well-educated," Sir Bale said dryly.

The Doctor gave a polite bow.

"But there's one thing you clearly don't understand."

"Oh? And what's that?" the Doctor asked.

"Medicine."

The Doctor laughed awkwardly. "Well—ha! You've got me there. I must admit, we missed the mark this time. But this is a one-of-a-kind case, I swear. It'll be talked about and written about, I promise. And when the papers come out, I'll make sure you see them."

"I won't read them," Sir Bale replied flatly. "Have another glass of sherry, Doctor."

The Doctor thanked him and poured another glass, lifting it toward the light.

"Ha! See that? Your port's so good it's stuck in my head. I keep looking for the beeswing like I'm holding a glass of it now."

But if he was hinting for more port, it didn't work. Sir Bale wasn't offering any.

"I assume Feltram's going to be fine," Sir Bale said. "If anything goes wrong, I'll call you—unless he dies again. In that case, I think I'll trust my own judgment."

With that, the two men parted ways.

Sir Bale didn't ask the Doctor about his own health, but he wasn't feeling great. "This miserable place, those awful mountains, and that dark, wet lake," he grumbled. "It's enough to drive anyone mad. Once your mood sinks, you're finished. That's why I have no appetite—it's that, and the cursed debt letters. I wish there was no mail service here at all. Back in Sir Amyrald's day, they shot a guy for trying to collect a debt, and no one said a word. Now they pelt you with letters from miles away and destroy whatever little peace you have in this wretched hole."

Was it gout? Depression? No one really knew. But Sir Bale's way of dealing with it was to go for long, tiring walks.

That evening, he went walking high up in the hills of Golden Friars. Though the valleys below had already faded into twilight, the slopes of the huge mountains were still lit by the soft, golden light of the setting sun.

There's no feeling quite like standing alone on a mountaintop. Far above the noise and clutter of everyday life, surrounded by the massive shapes of nature, a person can feel both small and strangely free. It's lonely in a way that's both peaceful and a little frightening—as if you've left behind all the normal rules of the world. The moon had started to rise behind him, casting a silver glow over the darkened landscape below. But Sir Bale still stood in the fading sun, which also lit up the tops of the distant Morvyn Fells across from him.

Sir Bale Mardykes didn't rush to climb down from the mountain, even though most people would've hurried while there was still some daylight left. He had known these quiet, remote hills since he was a boy, and besides, the thin moon hanging in the east would soon shine brighter as the sun disappeared, lighting his way like a lantern.

In the fading light, Sir Bale's strong, serious face had a look that reminded one of King Charles II—not the cheerful version from stories, but the darker, more intense version we see in old paintings.

He stood still on the slope with his arms crossed, taking in the view—even though he usually disliked it. The last light of the sun was coloring the far-off peaks, fading into deeper shades as night crept in. Down below, the outlines of Golden Friars and its tower were barely visible, with a few faint lights glowing in the windows.

As he stood there watching, the sun finally vanished and twilight fell quickly. He began to think about an old line from Homer describing how mountains and cliffs slowly appear in moonlight. To his right, a large white cloud that had been sitting on the mountaintops broke apart and started rolling down the hills like smoke from a cannon. Most of it spilled toward the lake, but some of it spread over the ground where he stood, wrapping everything in a heavy fog. It wasn't the thickest kind, though—he could still make out shapes of rocks and cliffs about thirty feet ahead.

Being caught alone in thick fog on a mountainside—especially one with cliffs—is deeply unsettling. It also messes with your imagination. Surrounded by mist, it's easy to picture something eerie or threatening creeping closer without warning.

Sir Bale wasn't worried about getting lost completely. He could feel the breeze from a certain direction, which helped him stay on track. But the fog was still thick enough to slow him down. As he turned to his left, trying to spot familiar landmarks, he suddenly saw a figure standing just a few yards away. The person was tall and thin, with one arm stretched out as if pointing at something far off—though no one could possibly see anything clearly in the fog.

Sir Bale stared, unsure if he was awake or dreaming. Where had this person come from? Before he could figure it out, the figure moved and disappeared.

He continued down the mountain slowly. The fog started to thin, and he could see a bit farther ahead now, which let him walk faster. But he still had a long way to go before he reached Mardykes Hall. The fog still blurred the view, but luckily he remembered the path from his childhood and didn't lose his way.

About four miles from home, he was walking under a rocky ledge called the Cat's Skaitch when he saw the same cloaked figure again, about thirty or forty yards ahead. The moonlight through the mist made the figure look ghostly and unreal.

Sir Bale stopped. The man nodded and stepped back, hiding behind the rock. Frustrated now, Sir Bale shouted for the stranger to stop and took off after him, moving quickly. But once again, the figure was gone, the mist making it easy to disappear.

As he made his way down toward Mardykes Hall, the mountains sloped into a steep, wooded glen. A narrow footpath cut through this ravine, leading to the flat land beside the lake. Sir Bale walked this rocky path under patches of moonlight, the air clearer now.

And just as he stepped onto the lower ground, he saw the same figure once more. This time, it came closer—and he saw clearly that it was Philip Feltram.

Chapter XIV.
A New Philip Feltram

Sir Bale Mardykes hadn't seen Philip Feltram since the strange night he came back to life. The last time they spoke, things had been tense—Sir Bale was cold and accusing, while Feltram had seemed hopeless and defeated.

Now Feltram stood in the moonlight, straight and tall, with a strange, sarcastic smile on his face. Something in his expression and posture made Sir Bale uneasy. This wasn't the broken man he'd last spoken to. He had planned to speak kindly when they next met, but the shock of seeing Feltram so suddenly threw him off. His voice came out sharp, just like it had during their last argument.

"I thought you were in bed, Mr. Feltram. I didn't expect to find you out here. I believe the doctor gave strict orders for you to rest."

"But I know better than the doctor," Feltram said, still smiling in that unsettling way.

"I think you'd be better off back in bed," Sir Bale said stiffly.

"Oh, come on," Feltram replied, brushing the comment off like it was nothing.

Sir Bale frowned. "You're forgetting yourself."

"It's easier to forget yourself than to forgive others sometimes," Feltram said, in a tone that was both bitter and calm.

"That's how fools make themselves sick," Sir Bale snapped. "You walked all the way to the Golden Friars hills, didn't you? I saw someone up there—it was you. That was foolish. What were you doing there?"

"I was watching you," Feltram answered flatly.

"You walked all the way there and back? How did you even get up there?"

"Oh, come on—how did I get there, how did you get there, how did the fog get there? We all come from the lake and go back again," he said with a smug look.

"You're talking nonsense," Sir Bale muttered.

"Yes," Feltram said, "but nonsense with a purpose."

Sir Bale stared at him. He wasn't sure if Feltram was being serious, or if something was wrong with him.

"I had planned to speak to you calmly," Sir Bale said, "but you seem to be making that hard." Feltram just kept smiling that same strange smile. "Honestly, I don't know what to make of you. Maybe you're sick. You must have walked nearly twelve miles."

"What an achievement," Feltram said sarcastically.

"It's a lot for someone who almost drowned," Sir Bale pointed out.

"Just a little dip," Feltram said. "You hate the lake, but I like it. When I touch the water, I come back stronger—like Antaeus touching the ground."

"I think you should go back inside and rest. Anyway, I wanted to tell you—there's no more trouble about that banknote."

"There isn't?" Feltram asked.

"No. Creswell came here last night and found it. I have it now, and you're not to blame," Sir Bale explained.

"But someone is to blame," Feltram said, still smiling.

"Well, it's not you, and that's all that matters," Sir Bale said firmly.

"That's it? That's how it ends? Really—how kind of you!" Feltram said, his voice dripping with sarcasm.

Sir Bale narrowed his eyes. There was something off about Feltram's tone—mocking, maybe even threatening. Before he could respond, Feltram spoke again.

"So we're all settled, you and I?"

"There's no reason you can't stay here at Mardykes now," Sir Bale said, trying to sound generous.

"I'll be here for two more years," Feltram said, glancing around with a dark, faraway look. "Then I'll go traveling."

Sir Bale frowned. Is he losing his mind? he wondered.

"But before I leave," Feltram said, "I have to help you figure out how to pay off your debts. That's why I'm here."

Sir Bale gave him a sharp look. This time, though, Feltram wasn't smiling in that cold, mocking way. His face looked serious—like he was hiding some inner pain.

"You'll understand everything soon enough," Feltram added.

Without saying anything else, and with a strange, unreadable expression, he walked off under the thick oak trees nearby. Sir Bale had the odd feeling that Feltram had been watching someone in the distance, and maybe he had seen a signal or sign that made him leave.

A few seconds later, Sir Bale followed, calling out after him. He didn't like the idea of Feltram wandering around in the dark, especially near cliffs or dangerous spots. If something happened to him again, it would only cause more trouble and shame for the family. But Feltram didn't answer, and in the dense woods, Sir Bale couldn't spot him again.

When he got back to Mardykes Hall, Sir Bale sent for Mrs. Julaper and had a long talk with her. But she couldn't say there was anything obviously wrong with Feltram. He just seemed more quiet than usual, as if he was keeping something to himself.

"But you know, Sir Bale," she said, "after everything he's been through, it's no surprise he's acting a little different. Facing death like that changes a man. I'm actually glad he's taking it seriously. I hope it really makes a difference in his life. Poor fellow—may it lead him to something better. Amen."

"Nice speech," said Sir Bale dryly, "but I don't think it's made him any better. If anything, he seems more strange and less at peace. I only asked you because I'm wondering if he might be sick—maybe has a fever or something. That would explain his odd behavior and give us a reason to go after him and bring him home to rest. But maybe you're right. Maybe the whole thing just shook him up, and he'll settle back to normal in a few days."

But that's not what happened. The change in Philip Feltram didn't go away—it got stronger over time. It wasn't just his mood that changed. His whole appearance shifted too. He became thinner. His eyes sank into dark hollows, and his face started to look harsh and distant.

His behavior changed too. He acted completely different toward Sir Bale. People even started saying that the Baronet, who used to boss

Feltram around and treat him like a servant, now seemed a little afraid of him.

And the strangest part? Somehow, Feltram had gained real power over Sir Bale—someone who once looked down on him with total disdain.

Chapter XV.
The Purse of Gold

Sir Bale Mardykes didn't know many people in the area. He kept to himself, rarely socialized, and didn't invite others to his home. He was dealing with large debts, and because he was proud, he avoided people rather than admit how bad things were. He liked people to think he was carefully managing his estate—but the truth was, the estate wasn't improving at all. In fact, people around the countryside knew just how little he was able to do. Everyone understood that all he could manage was to pay off the interest and live in a very modest way.

The lake stretched about four or five miles from the small dock by Mardykes Hall to a place called Cloostedd. Philip Feltram, who had become quiet and gloomy, had taken to rowing out on the lake by himself. Sometimes he would spend the entire day alone in the little sailboat, even handling it all on his own. He often went to Cloostedd, where he would tie up the boat beneath the tall, shadowy trees that reflected on the dark water. Then he'd disappear into the woods. People guessed he was walking there to dwell on old family wrongs—remembering past mistreatment and holding on to his growing anger and silence.

One evening in the fall, Sir Bale sat alone after dinner, feeling grumpy. The sunset poured bright red light across the valley at the far end of the lake, coloring the otherwise dark water and shining on the sail of Feltram's boat as he returned from his lonely trip.

"There comes my gloomy ghost of a housemate," Sir Bale muttered, slouched back in his big chair. "What a joyful life—dreary house, miserable people, and a future worth nothing. This place would drive anyone mad—and it has, that idiot included."

He looked away from the window, trying to push the thought aside. Instead, he started thinking about the horse races coming up next week at Heckleston Downs. Lots of money would change hands there, and it frustrated him that he couldn't even take part.

Just then, Mrs. Julaper stepped into the room. "Ah, Mrs. Julaper—is that you?" he said.

She gave a small curtsy and said, "I came to ask if you'd like a jug of mulled claret, sir."

"No, not really," he said. "I'll just have a mug of beer and my pipe. That's more fitting for a man who's broke."

"You're not broke, sir," she replied quickly. "You're no worse off than half the lords and big men in the country. I wouldn't let anyone else say that about you."

"That's kind of you, Mrs. Julaper, but I won't argue with myself, especially since it's true—damn true. Look here, every Mardykes before me could bet a hundred or a thousand pounds at Heckleston. What could I bet now? A mug of beer, if I'm lucky. It was my great-grandfather who started the races, and now I can't even show my face there. Well, what can I do? Just deal with it, I suppose. You know what—yes, bring me that claret after all. I'll smoke my pipe first. Bring it in an hour."

After she left, he lit his pipe and went to the window, staring out at the sky, which was slowly fading to gray.

He finished smoking as it got darker, and he stayed by the window, staring into the night. His thoughts grew bitter. He imagined how even a little good luck at the races could change his life, while so many others who didn't need it would win big. Like the dark landscape outside, his thoughts were gloomy and cloudy, filled with anger and selfish frustration.

"How many thousands will change hands at Heckleston next week—and not a single coin will come my way," he muttered. "There are men who would sell their souls just to know who's going to win. At least the devil has sense—he doesn't cheat himself."

Something moved. He noticed a shadow on the wall. The firelight flickered, casting a huge shape on the wall behind him—someone was standing there. A hand rested on his shoulder.

Startled, Sir Bale spun around and saw Philip Feltram standing there, his face hard and serious, eyes intense. He didn't move his hand from the Baronet's shoulder, and his stare was sharp and strange.

"Feltram! You startled me," said Sir Bale. "It feels like I only just saw your boat out on the lake—and now you're here already. Ha! Time does fly. You really surprised me. Would you like something to drink? I'll ring for a glass."

"You've been worried about those debts," Feltram said flatly. "I told you I'd take care of them, didn't I?"

There was a long pause. Sir Bale stared at Feltram's face. If this had happened somewhere else—somewhere brighter and less eerie—he might have laughed. But here, alone in Mardykes, the place had worn him down. He was jumpy and anxious.

He forced a smile and shook his head sadly. "That's kind of you, Feltram. I know you mean well. You'd help me if you could."

As Sir Bale said the words "kind" and "kindness," Feltram's strange smile grew more intense with each repetition. It made Sir Bale feel worse the longer it went on. Then, just as suddenly, Feltram's face turned cold again.

"I found a fortune-teller in Cloostedd Wood," he said. "Here—look at this."

He pulled a leather purse from his pocket and dropped it on the table. Sir Bale heard the coins inside.

"A fortune-teller? Don't tell me she gave you that," Sir Bale said, surprised.

Feltram smiled and nodded. "It used to be the fortune-teller who got a coin. This one gave me money."

"Well that's a new twist," said Sir Bale, sounding more like his old self. "She gave you money instead of taking it?"

Feltram's smile deepened. "It wasn't a 'she.' He gave it to me—with a message."

"Oh, so it was a man," said Sir Bale, raising an eyebrow.

"Gypsies usually travel in groups—men and women together," said Feltram. "Maybe he lent the money, even if she was the one telling fortunes."

"That's the first time I've ever heard of a gypsy lending money," Sir Bale said, raising his eyebrows and eyeing the purse with a crooked smile.

Feltram, still holding the purse with his thin fingers, sat down at the table. His expression tightened like he was deep in some sly thought. He leaned back and lowered his chin to his chest.

"I always thought," Sir Bale went on, "that ever since ancient Egypt was conquered, the Egyptians avoided lending and left that job to the Jews."

Feltram suddenly looked up. "What would you give to know who's going to win at the Heckleston races?"

"That would definitely be worth something," said Sir Bale, now watching Feltram more closely. He sounded casual, but he was clearly paying attention.

"I could lend you the money to place your bet," Feltram said, his voice quiet but sharp.

"You're serious?" asked Sir Bale, suddenly more alert. His tone, posture, and face changed with interest.

"There's weight in that purse," Feltram replied with a strange smile. He lifted it a little and dropped it onto the table with a loud clink.

"Well, whatever it is—it's real," said Sir Bale, staring at it.

Feltram turned the purse upside down and poured out a shining pile of gold guineas onto the table.

"You're telling me a gypsy gave you all this in Cloostedd Wood?" Sir Bale asked, amazed.

"A friend gave it to me," Feltram said. "A friend who is... me."

"You? Then it's yours? You're lending it?" said Sir Bale, stunned. He couldn't take his eyes off the pile of gold. He had no idea how Feltram, who'd never had a penny to his name, could suddenly have so much money.

"Myself... but not exactly myself," Feltram said in a strange, mysterious way. "Like a man and his shadow. Or a voice and its echo."

Sir Bale stared at him, trying to figure out what he meant. Then something old popped into his mind—an old story he'd heard as a child.

There had once been two Feltram brothers who lived in Cloostedd long ago. They had joined the king's army during the civil war and were said to have buried a fortune—gold, jewels, and silver—in the woods. They told one loyal servant the hiding place. But not long after, both brothers were killed at the Battle of Marston Moor, and the servant died of a fever soon after. No one ever found the treasure. Over the years, treasure hunters dug under trees and beside large rocks all over the forest, but nothing was ever discovered. Eventually, people stopped searching. The tale became just a bedtime story.

Now that story rushed back into Sir Bale's mind. The only explanation he could think of for Feltram having so much gold was that he had found the long-lost treasure during one of his lonely walks.

"Maybe those gypsies found the gold in the same spot where you found them," said Sir Bale. "And since Cloostedd Forest and everything in it belongs to me, it's less of a gift and more like them handing me my own coat when I ask for it."

Feltram looked at him coldly. "Don't be foolish, Sir Bale. Don't trust the law too much and refuse help just because it wasn't requested. If you like being in debt, then fine—keep your mortgages. But if you want my help, take the offer. I won't beg. Think it over and tell me when you're ready."

He swept the gold coins back into the purse, stuffed it deep into the pocket of his coat, and left the room, muttering to himself as he went.

Chapter XVI.
The Message from Cloostedd

"Come back, Feltram! Philip, come back!" Sir Bale called quickly. "Let's talk this over, can't we? You must have misunderstood me. I'd really like to hear the whole story."

"It's not much of a story, sir," Feltram said as he came back into the room, only half closing the door behind him. "Earlier today in Cloostedd Forest, I met some people. One of them could tell the future. He told me the winners of the first three races at Heckleston and gave me this purse, letting me lend you as much as you want to bet on the races. No strings attached. You won't owe anything unless you go looking for him."

"Well, that sounds like a fair deal," said Sir Bale, glancing longingly at the purse Feltram had placed on the table again.

"Not bad at all," Feltram repeated in a flat, low voice.

"You'll tell me the names of the winners, won't you?" asked Sir Bale. "I'd like to know."

"I'll tell you if you come for a walk with me," said Feltram.

"Why not just tell me here?" asked Sir Bale.

"My memory works better out there. Some people, in some places, even if they don't say a word, seem to block your thoughts. Come on— let's talk," Feltram said, leading the way.

Sir Bale shrugged and followed him.

By now it was completely dark. Feltram walked slowly toward the edge of the lake, and Sir Bale followed, getting more curious the longer the walk lasted. He gave a faint smile as he looked at Feltram's tall, skinny shape in front of him—almost like he was pretending to mock him, even though deep down he wasn't feeling amused at all.

When they got to the lake's edge, Feltram crouched down. It looked like he was talking to someone lying there, maybe even stroking them. Sir Bale thought he saw a dark figure stretched out in the shallow water, but as he got closer, he realized it was just a shadow on the lake. It disappeared when he moved, and Feltram was only swishing his hand in the water and quietly muttering to himself. When Sir Bale reached him, Feltram stood up and said:

"I like listening to the water ripple through the grass and pebbles. The lake whispers everywhere along the shore. Just poetic nonsense— but you're such a romantic, I'm sure you'll forgive me."

There was a sharpness in his eyes, a bitter smile, and a tone that made Sir Bale feel insulted. But he didn't show it. Even if he hadn't been so curious, he probably wouldn't have let it show. He didn't like to admit it, but Feltram was gaining some kind of power over him, and it made him uneasy.

"You're not to tell anyone," Feltram said, stepping closer in the dark. "The secret's yours once you promise."

"Of course I promise," said Sir Bale. "If I believed it, I'd be an idiot to tell; and if I didn't, I wouldn't waste my time."

Feltram crouched again, scooped some water into the palm of his hand, and said, "Now, you do the same. Cup your hand like this. I'll split the water—half for me, half for you." He poured part of the water into Sir Bale's palm. Sir Bale watched with a nervous smile, mocking the ritual but feeling strangely unsure.

"Now promise me you won't reveal anything about the one who told me or how I found out—no matter who it is."

"Yes, I promise," said Sir Bale.

"Now do what I do," Feltram said. He let the water fall to the ground and used his damp fingers to touch his forehead and chest. Then he reached out and joined hands with Sir Bale. "There—you're bound to secrecy."

Sir Bale laughed. "That reminds me of that old game—what's it called? Grand Mufti?"

"Exactly," Feltram said. "It means nothing... except that someday, you might remember it and it will matter." Then, after standing silently for a moment, he added, "Now, the names. Don't speak—just listen, or you might break the spell. The winner of the first race is Beeswing. The second, Falcon. The third, Lightning."

He spoke slowly and quietly, as though it took effort to remember. His eyes were closed, and his arms were lifted slightly, fingers stretched, like he was searching through darkness. He let out sighs and faint groans as he spoke, like someone about to fall asleep—or pass out. When he finished, he stood there, swaying slightly, mumbling to himself like a man who'd been through something exhausting. He looked like someone on the edge of death.

Eventually, he opened his eyes, glanced around with a dazed, almost wild look, sighed deeply, and sat down on a big rock near the lake. He sighed again, and again—like a man recovering from some huge physical strain.

After a long pause, Sir Bale finally spoke. "You know... I wish I could believe you. But your list is just too crazy. Not one of those horses has the slightest chance. Not one!"

"That's better for you," Feltram replied. "You'll get great odds. Take advantage of your luck. Beeswing runs on Tuesday." He tapped his chest, where he had placed the purse. "If you need money, I'll be your banker—this is your bank."

Then he turned and walked off quickly.

Sir Bale stood there, watching him vanish into the darkness. His thoughts were a mess. Was Feltram crazy? Was he trying to pull off a trick? Or had he actually gone to some fortune-telling gypsies and taken their predictions seriously? Where had the gold come from? That was the biggest question of all.

Maybe, Sir Bale thought, the old Trebecks—wealthy mountain shepherds who liked Feltram—had given him the money. Maybe Feltram was pretending it was for himself, but really meant it as a loan for him. That made some sense, at least.

Whatever the case, Sir Bale decided he'd go ahead and use the gold. The risk seemed small, and the reward—if he picked the right horse— might be everything he needed.

Around eleven o'clock, Feltram walked straight into Sir Bale's library without being announced. He didn't take off his hat and sat down across the table, staring gloomily at Sir Bale for a while.

"Are you still planning to use the purse?" he finally asked.

"Of course," said Sir Bale eagerly. "I always need a purse."

"The deal is this," Feltram said. "You have to bet on all three horses I named. You can bet as much or as little as you like, but at least five pounds out of every hundred must be placed on each one. That's the rule. If you break it, you'll upset some powerful people—and you'll regret it. Do you agree?"

"Sure. Five pounds per hundred—no problem," Sir Bale said. "So how many hundreds are we talking about?"

"Three," Feltram replied.

"Well, a guy with good luck might win something with three hundred pounds, but it's not exactly a fortune."

"It's more than enough—if you use it right," said Feltram.

"Three hundred pounds," Sir Bale repeated as he poured the coins out of the purse Feltram had just handed him. He began separating them into small piles of twenty-five, looking at the gold with serious focus. He didn't even think to thank Feltram—his mind was on the money, not the person who gave it.

"Yeah," he said after counting again, "it's exactly three hundred. So I need to bet five pounds on each of those three horses... that's fifteen pounds total. What a waste to bet on those weird horses you mentioned—but I guess if I have to, I have to." He said it like he was hoping to be talked out of it.

"If you don't, you'll be sorry," Feltram said coldly, then turned and walked out.

"There's an old saying," Sir Bale muttered with a grin, "'A penny in your pocket is a cheerful companion.'" As he dropped the gold coins back into the purse, he felt better than he had in a long time.

It had been ages since he'd been to a racetrack or anywhere fun. But now, with money in his hand, he could go out in public again without worrying about being embarrassed. He could finally enjoy the thrill of betting and winning.

"Who knows how this might turn out?" he thought. "My luck has to turn eventually. Last summer in Germany, last winter in Paris—hell, life owes me something. It's about time I won big."

Sir Bale had gotten used to a slow, lonely life full of grumbling and frustration. But now, he knew he had to look sharp for the races. He didn't want people thinking he was broke. So he made sure everything he wore and carried looked just right.

That Monday, with his groom riding behind him, Sir Bale left for the Saracen's Head inn in Heckleston, where he would stay during the races. He looked just as polished and well-dressed as any nobleman could hope to be.

Chapter XVII.
On the Course—Beeswing, Falcon, and Lightning

As Sir Bale rode toward Golden Friars early in the morning, the last bits of fog were fading. He looked back at Mardykes with a sense of hope—hope that he'd soon leave that gloomy place behind and return to the exciting life he loved in Europe. The sun lit up the edges of the old house, casting a warm glow on its rooftops. The tall trees around it looked proud and still, while the hills behind stayed dark, turning away from the rising sun. Down below, in the steep Feltram valley that led to the lake, the soft morning light was just starting to shine through the shadows. Out on the water, he spotted a small white sail—Feltram's boat—already gliding halfway between Mardykes and the quiet, wooded shores of Cloostedd.

"Off on the same mission, I'd bet," Sir Bale thought. "I hope he's lucky. Yes, he's headed for Cloostedd Forest. Maybe he'll find his gipsies there again—those Trebecks, or whoever they are."

Feeling a bit ashamed of relying on such people, he told himself, "Who cares? Lots of guys walk away rich from Heckleston with less than this. Paying them back won't be hard if I win big."

He passed through Golden Friars on horseback. Some people who didn't like him made snide comments about his flashy appearance, wondered how he paid for it, and joked that he must be out looking for a rich wife. Still, many were impressed by how sharp he looked. It was rare to see their Baronet so well turned out, and the change made people talk—in a good way.

The next day, Sir Bale was at the Heckleston racecourse. He was catching up with old acquaintances and trying to be charming, while others watched him with curiosity and interest. After some time socializing near the fancy carriages, he left the ladies and headed straight for the betting crowd—ready for serious business.

Did he keep his promise? Yes, he did. He placed bets on Beeswing, Falcon, and Lightning—just as Feltram had said. But only the bare minimum: five guineas each, exactly what he had agreed to. The odds were awful—forty-five to one against Beeswing, sixty to one against Lightning, and fifty to one against Falcon.

"What a joke!" Sir Bale grumbled. "Like I have so much money lying around that I can afford to throw it away!"

He was annoyed, feeling like Feltram's tip had been ridiculous and the money was his to begin with.

So how did it turn out?

By the end of the week, Sir Bale was riding away from Heckleston in a bad mood. He was angry at his luck and not too happy with himself. Still—he had won. The race results were strange. The favorites all lost: one due to an accident, another on a technical rule, and the third fair and square. And the winners? Exactly the horses that Feltram's "fortune-teller" had named.

So how much did he win? Just 775 guineas. Not bad—but if he'd bet 100 guineas on each horse instead of five, he would've taken home 15,500 guineas.

He arrived at Mardykes feeling like a man who had lost nearly 15,000 pounds. When he got off his horse at the front door, he found Feltram waiting there. Feltram gave a dry little laugh.

"What are you laughing at?" Sir Bale snapped.

"You won, didn't you?" Feltram asked.

"Yes, I won. A little."

"On the horses I told you about?"

"Well, yeah… but it was just luck," Sir Bale said with irritation.

Feltram gave another quiet laugh and turned away.

Sir Bale entered the house, feeling more sour than he had before the trip. Days passed, and something started bothering him: Feltram never brought up the money again. It was strange, really. The whole thing had been almost unbelievable. No talk of paying it back, even though Sir Bale had made hundreds from it. And somehow, those three exact horses had won.

Who was this fortune-teller, really? Sir Bale started seriously thinking about finding him—maybe even inviting him to stay near Mardykes, giving his people a place to camp, and offering them chickens or a pig now and then. That mysterious man could be worth more than gold—he might be able to make Sir Bale rich in no time. And if Bale didn't act soon, someone else probably would.

Tired of waiting for Feltram to bring it up again, Sir Bale decided to start the conversation himself. He hadn't seen Feltram for two or three days, but now he spotted him in the woods near Mardykes. Feltram was standing on a small hill among thick trees, leaning on a walking stick he sometimes used on long walks.

"Feltram!" Sir Bale shouted.

Feltram turned and waved for him to come closer. Sir Bale grumbled a little under his breath but walked over anyway.

"I brought you here," Feltram said, "because from this spot today, you can clearly see the opening of Feltram's Glen across the lake, and that group of trees where you'll find the path to the man you keep thinking about."

"Who says I'm always thinking about him?" snapped Sir Bale. He felt like Feltram had caught him in a weakness, and it made him defensive.

"I say it," Feltram replied calmly, "because I know it's true. And so do you. Look at that bunch of trees down in the hollow. On the left, there's an old oak tree. Carved into the bark are two large letters—H and F. The cuts are so deep, time hasn't worn them away. If you stand with your back to those letters, you'll be looking straight up into Feltram's Glen. Ahead of you lies Cloostedd Forest, wide and thick. Now, what do you think about our fortune-teller?"

"That's what I want to find out," Sir Bale answered. "I'm not saying he's magical, but he either made a crazy lucky guess or he has some real source of information. Maybe it's part guessing, part facts. Either way, I think he's remarkable. I'd like to meet him, talk with him, maybe even set something up so I can ask for his advice again."

"I think he's willing to meet you," Feltram said. "But he's stubborn and strange. He won't come to you—you'll have to go to him. And you have to approach the way he wants, or you might not find him at all. That's part of the deal."

Sir Bale laughed. "He knows his value and wants to set the rules."

"Well, that's fair," said Feltram. "If you still want to meet him, here's how: Stand with your back to the letters carved into the oak tree. In front of you is an old Druid altar stone. Look closely. Somewhere on it, there will be a dark stain, about the size of a person's head. Its location changes daily. From where you stand, that mark will point you in the direction you need to go. Use the trees and landmarks in that line to guide you. And when the forest gets thick, do your best to stay on course. That's the path to him."

"You should come with me," said Sir Bale. "I'll probably get lost out there and never find the guy."

"When two people want to meet, they usually do," Feltram replied. "I'll go part of the way with you. I can walk with you through the forest until I start seeing a small flower that grows only along the paths those people take. When I see it, I'll have to turn back. But first, I'll row you across the lake."

"No way," Sir Bale said quickly. "I'm not going over that lake."

"But that's how the fortune-teller wants to be approached," Feltram said.

"I've had a strange feeling about that lake since I was a child," Sir Bale admitted. "Old stories and warnings stuck with me. I know it's silly, but I can't shake it. I'd rather ride around."

"But it's twenty-five miles around the lake," Feltram warned. "And even if you made the trip, he still wouldn't meet you. He wants it done his way."

"The sun's almost down," he added. "See that dead branch near Snakes Island? It looks like fingers sticking out of the water. When those tips turn red, the sun has only three minutes left."

"I can't see it from here," Sir Bale said. "It's too far."

"Yes," Feltram replied. "The lake has signs—but not everyone can see them."

"That's true," Sir Bale muttered. "Still, I'll ride there. That's how I'll do it this time."

"Then you won't find him," Feltram said. "And he wants his money. You don't want to make him angry."

"You're the one who borrowed the money," said Sir Bale.

"Yes," Feltram agreed.

"Well then, it's your job to pay him back," said Sir Bale firmly.

"Maybe," Feltram said. "But he invited you. If you don't go, he might be insulted. You may never hear from him again."

"Well, we'll see. When can you go?" asked Sir Bale. "The Langton races are coming up next week. For once, I don't mind trying my luck. What do you think?"

"You can go pay him yourself," Feltram replied. "Ask him who's going to win. The whole county will be there, and a lot of money will be made."

"I'll give it a shot," said Sir Bale.

"When will you go?" asked Feltram.

"Tomorrow," he replied.

"I've got a strange feeling, Feltram," said Sir Bale, gently placing his hand on Feltram's arm, "that you're really going to help me get rid of those awful mortgages."

Feltram replied coldly, "So do I." Then he turned and walked down the hill without another word or look back.

Chapter XVIII.
On the Lake, at Last

The next day, Philip Feltram rowed across the lake. Sir Bale saw the little boat and instantly guessed where it was going. He watched closely as it moved toward the rough dock at the mouth of Feltram's Glen. That was all the proof he needed—Feltram was off to meet the fortune-teller again, likely trying to get another prediction before the upcoming race.

That evening, Feltram came back. Later, he walked into Sir Bale's library. The Baronet felt more relieved—and curious—than he wanted to admit.

Feltram noticed right away and didn't waste any time.

"I spent nearly the whole day in Cloostedd Forest," he said. "The old man was furious. He didn't offer me anything, not even a drink. He was mad that you wouldn't cross the lake to speak to him yourself. He took the money you sent, counted it, stuffed it in his pocket—and then cursed your name. Still, I managed to calm him down, and in the end, he talked."

"What did he say?" asked Sir Bale.

"He said the Mardykes estate will one day belong to a Feltram."

"Well, he could've said something a little more believable," Sir Bale muttered. "Did he say anything else?"

"Yes. He said the winning horse at Langton Lea would be Silver Bell."

"No other picks?"

"No."

"Silver Bell? That's not as crazy as the last prediction. That horse actually has good odds. A lot of people are betting on it. I wouldn't mind backing Silver Bell."

Truthfully, the moment Sir Bale heard the name, he had already made up his mind. This time, he was going all in.

On race day, he felt confident. Some parts of his land still hadn't been sold, and his name still carried weight. People were happy to take his bets. Caught up in the excitement, he ended up betting nearly twenty thousand pounds on Silver Bell. If the horse won, he'd make seven thousand pounds more.

But Silver Bell lost. Sir Bale lost everything.

Now the Mardykes estate was in serious danger. Sir Bale returned from the races a mess, with piles of IOUs and no plan.

Feltram was waiting at the steps of Mardykes Hall again, just like last time. The evening sun stretched his shadow far across the ground, all the way toward the lake. As Sir Bale approached, Feltram gave a dry laugh.

This time, Sir Bale was too beaten down to argue.

He glared at Feltram but said nothing until he got off his horse.

"Last time, you didn't trust the old man," said Feltram. "This time, he didn't trust you. He was angry—so he gave you the wrong horse."

"It wasn't his fault. I would've bet on that stupid horse anyway," Sir Bale growled. "Some prophet you've found. Maybe he's right about one thing—if a Feltram had money, they could take this place. But they don't. They're all broke. So much for your fortune-teller."

"He might still help you," Feltram said, "if you're willing to make peace."

"That fraud? What can he do now? I'm finished."

"Don't talk like that," said Feltram. "Show some respect. He can still help you—he forgives, if you approach him the right way. I've heard your situation is getting worse. You should go fix it."

"Fix it? With someone who can't even predict a race right? Why should I bother?"

"He doesn't like being ignored," said Feltram. "You offended him. He won't speak to you unless you go his way."

"If that's what he's waiting for, he'll be waiting forever. I'm not crossing that lake by boat," Sir Bale said firmly.

But as his debts piled up and pressure mounted, Sir Bale started to change his mind. Everything was collapsing.

"I don't see why it matters if I ride around the lake instead of taking a boat," he said.

Feltram gave him a strange smile. "I don't know. Do you?"

"Of course not," snapped Sir Bale. "And who is he to tell me how I should travel? It's ridiculous. And clearly, he can't even predict the future. Do you seriously believe in him?"

"I do," said Feltram. "He tricked you on purpose. He likes to teach lessons to people who don't respect him. He's not spiteful—he usually has a reason. Now he's forcing you to come to him, and when you do, I believe he'll help. That's what he told me."

"So you saw him again?"

"Yesterday," Feltram said. "He's pushing you—but he still wants to help."

"If he really wants to help, tell him I don't need a fortune-teller. I need a banker. Let him give me another loan, like before."

"He'll do it," said Feltram. "Once he's on your side, he stays there."

"There's another race coming up at Byermere. I could win it all back. But it's nearly a month away. What am I supposed to do in the meantime?"

"Everyone's got to handle their own problems," Feltram said coldly. "I'm not like you."

Sir Bale's anxiety got worse. Creditors were demanding money fast. The market was bad, and selling land was harder than ever.

"All I can tell them is that I'm selling property. That takes time! I've got enough to pay everyone—twice. Back in the day, people used to wait for gentlemen to sell their land. Damn it, what more do they want? My soul?"

In the end, less than a week later, Sir Bale gave in. He told Feltram he would cross the lake by boat—just like the old man wanted. He didn't even care if he drowned doing it.

It was a beautiful autumn day. The sun cast a golden glow over everything. The deep blue lake shimmered with light. In the distance, cliffs and trees stood clear against the soft, warm sky.

Sir Bale hadn't been feeling well. The night before, he'd sent for Doctor Torvey. The doctor hadn't been available, but he arrived that morning—right when Sir Bale was about to leave. He stopped him in the courtyard for a quick check-up.

"You should be in bed," the doctor said. "You're crazy to be out like this. Your pulse is way too high. If you cross that lake and walk around Cloostedd, you'll be out of your mind by the time you come back."

Sir Bale gave a quiet apology, like his life meant more to the doctor than it did to him. He promised to take it easy, said the air would do him good, and insisted he had no choice. So the doctor let him go.

Sir Bale climbed into the boat next to Feltram. The sail was raised, and the soft breeze from Golden Friars filled it. The boat pulled away from the dock beneath Mardykes Hall. The journey had begun.

Chapter XIX.
Mystagogus

The sail dropped, and the boat bumped gently against the stone step. Feltram hopped out and tied the boat to an old iron ring. Sir Bale followed behind. So—that was it. He had crossed the lake, and nothing bad had happened. He stood there, looking around like he was dreaming. He hadn't been to this place since he was a child. There was no sadness or guilt—just a sudden rush of old memories, as if time had never passed at all.

The little valley where they stood, the three hawthorn trees on the right—every curve in the grassy ground, every crack in the mossy rock below—came back to him instantly and clearly.

"Your brother and I used to fish for hours over there, by that bramble bush," Sir Bale said, pointing. "It looks exactly the same—not a single change. We'd eat blackberries right off it, with our fishing rods stuck in the dirt. It was later in the season than now, I think. After a few days, we had picked it clean. The steward used to come around— they were marking trees to be cut, walking through the woods with axes. I wonder what happened to that old boat. I haven't seen it since we came back. It was over in the woods to the right—that side's called the forest. People say it used to stretch for eight miles up the lakeshore and was filled with deer. There used to be a forester and some kind of ranger, all that official stuff. Your brother was older than you, right? He went off to India—or somewhere far. Is he still alive?"

"I don't care," Feltram said flatly.

"Well, that's a cold thing to say. But do you even know?"

"No, and why should I? If he's alive, I'm sure he's got his own problems—working hard, barely getting by. And if he's dead, he's rotting in the ground and probably stinks."

Sir Bale stared at him. Not long ago, Feltram had cried just talking about his brother. Now he looked cold and harsh, with a twisted little smile.

"You're joking, right?" Sir Bale asked.

"No. I'm being honest. You'd say the same thing if you were, too. If he's alive, he can stay wherever he is. And if he's dead, I want nothing to do with him—not his body, not his spirit. Do you hear that?"

"That sound? Like wind in the trees?"

"Yeah."

"But I don't feel any wind. The leaves aren't even moving."

"I noticed that too," Feltram said. "Come on."

He started walking up the gentle slope of the glen. Bits of rock poked up through the grass, and patches of ferns and thorny bushes made the place look wild and forgotten. In the distance, the path curved out of view behind a hill covered in trees.

They walked in silence toward a group of trees Feltram had pointed out earlier from the other side of the lake.

As they got closer, the trees appeared more spaced out than they'd looked from far away. Two or three were much taller and thicker than Sir Bale had expected. To the left, the wide valley of Cloostedd Forest opened up, with scattered trees here and there. As the land sloped downward, the trees grew thicker and formed a large, quiet forest—still and glowing with autumn colors.

What happened next is strange. Everything that follows comes from Sir Bale Mardykes himself. He told the same story every time, and all the details matched. Still, he was sick and feverish, so people are free to doubt what he said.

As they got close to the trees, a huge bird—something like a giant parrot—burst out from the branches and flew off. It flapped low over the grass, sometimes landing, then flying again. It stuck close to the little stream that flowed from the forest through the glen. The bird kept jumping and fluttering like its wing was hurt, and it screeched the whole time.

"That must be Mrs. Amerald's bird—the one that flew off last week," said Sir Bale, stopping to watch it. "Wasn't it a macaw?"

"No," Feltram answered. "That was a gray parrot. But there are stranger birds in Cloostedd Forest. My ancestors collected all kinds of birds that could survive the weather here. They gave them the right food and shelter until they got used to it. That's why there are so many unusual ones still around."

"Wow, that's a secret worth knowing," said Sir Bale. "That would really be something. What a fat bird that was—green, red, and yellow, with a white head. I guess that's from age. And that broken beak—ugly thing! But amazing feathers. It looked like a mix between a parrot and a vulture."

He was joking, but his interest was real. When he was younger, he had enjoyed birdwatching, and for a moment, he forgot all his troubles and the real reason he was out here.

Just then, another bird took off from the same tree. It was long and thin, completely white, and flew toward the forest.

"Looks like a kite, but its body's a little too long, isn't it?" said Sir Bale, pausing to watch it.

"Probably a foreign kind," said Feltram.

Nearby, a jay was hopping around them, not afraid of people. It seemed used to this quiet place. It tilted its head and looked at them curiously, pecked at the ground, and hopped around them in a circle. Then it flew up and landed on a branch of the old oak tree—the same one the other birds had come from. After a moment, it fluttered down onto a large flat stone that looked like an ancient table. The bird strutted across it like it was performing on stage. Then, with a quick jump, it flew off in the same direction as the other birds and disappeared into the forest.

"This is the tree," said Feltram.

"I remember it," said Sir Bale. "It's huge. And yes, those marks— I never noticed they were letters before. H and F—how strange I didn't see it. They're huge, but the shapes are so stretched and filled in oddly, and the moss has grown around them. I probably just thought they were natural cracks in the bark."

"Easy mistake," said Feltram.

Sir Bale had noticed since they left the shore that Feltram seemed to be changing—growing darker, more intense, and strange. His face looked harder, more serious, and full of shadows. The quiet, wild setting and the unsettling mood of his companion were beginning to make Sir Bale nervous.

They both stood silently, side by side, staring out at the forest. In front of them, the ground was dotted with large trees and twisted groups of birch and thorn, spread out in a natural, uneven way.

"Now stand between the letters," said Feltram suddenly in a low, serious voice. It startled Sir Bale.

He turned and realized he had, by chance, positioned himself exactly between the large letters H and F carved into the tree. From there, he could look out straight toward Cloostedd Forest.

"Yeah, I'm in the right spot," said Sir Bale.

Inside, he felt a strange mix of excitement and unease, like a soldier about to enter battle. Feltram's stern look and dark mood made him even more unsettled.

"Look closely at the stone," Feltram said. "See if you can spot a black mark about the size of your hand anywhere on it."

Sir Bale didn't act doubtful now. His imagination had been stirred, and something about all this felt oddly real.

"Do you see it?" asked Feltram.

Sir Bale stared, but he didn't see anything unusual.

Feltram's expression grew darker and more intense. He stepped away and walked in circles around the tree, clenching his fists and pacing like someone trying to warm up on a cold day. He looked frustrated and impatient. Then he came back to the stone and stared at it again.

Sir Bale kept watching. Then he frowned, squinted, and said, "Wait... yeah... hold on. There it is. It's getting clearer."

It didn't look like a shadow. Instead, it seemed like the stone was becoming see-through, and something dark—like a hand—was rising just under the surface. It slowly became sharper, and then it stopped moving. It looked like it was pointing toward the forest.

"It looks like a hand," said Sir Bale. "Yeah—it is a hand, pointing toward the forest."

"Forget the finger," said Feltram. "Just look at the black shape. From where you're standing, use that direction to find a landmark— like a tree—and walk toward it. Once you reach the forest, try to keep that same path. Look for small flowers with leaves like wood-sorrel and tall, thin stems. The blossoms are tiny and red, like a drop of blood. You've never seen them before. Follow the trail where they grow thickest. That's how you'll find him."

While Feltram was explaining, Sir Bale tried to spot something to guide him. Finally, he fixed his eyes on a lonely ash tree, one of its thick branches snapped by lightning. The bare white wood looked like fingers pointing toward the forest.

"Got it," said Sir Bale. "Come with me part of the way."

Feltram didn't answer. He just shook his head slowly, turned around, and walked away, leaving Sir Bale on his own.

That strange humming sound they'd heard earlier from the woods was gone now. The air was completely still. Not a bird was in sight. Not a sound, not a movement—just deep, heavy silence.

It would have been silly to back out now. Feltram had disappeared behind some bushes. Alone now, full of a strange new curiosity, Sir Bale stepped forward to find out where this path would lead.

Chapter XX.
The Haunted Forest

Sir Bale Mardykes walked straight ahead, stepping over bushes and rocky patches as he crossed the uneven ground toward the dead ash tree. As he got closer, its twisted, lifeless branch stretched high into the air, pointing toward the forest like a sign. He passed it, and soon it was out of sight behind him. He kept walking, now under the thick shade of the woods, carefully following the path Feltram had told him to take. Every now and then, after picking out a landmark to guide him, he would pause and look around to stay on course.

When he was a boy, he'd never gone this deep into the woods. He wasn't allowed—adults were afraid he'd get lost or stuck there after dark. He'd also heard spooky stories that the forest was haunted, which kept him away. That's why the place felt so unfamiliar and mysterious now. Sometimes the trees opened up in long, empty paths where he could see far into the shadows. He didn't see any flowers except for a few wild anemones and patches of wood-sorrel here and there.

As he went deeper, huge oak trees began to appear more often, until they made up nearly the whole forest. The tree trunks were wide and bent slightly at the bottom, like pillars holding up a dark, leafy ceiling high above.

Walking through these towering oaks, something caught his eye. A strange little flower was growing alone at the root of one of the trees. He bent down and picked it. Just as he did, a loud screech burst out above him, and a large bird with heavy flapping wings flew off through the branches. He didn't get a good look, but the scream reminded him of the big macaw he'd seen before.

The flower was odd. Its stem was thin as a thread, holding up a small, bell-shaped blossom that looked like a drop of blood and trembled constantly. He kept walking, holding it between his fingers. Soon he saw another just like it, and then another. They began to appear more often—some to the right, some to the left—until the ground ahead was scattered with the trembling red flowers. As he walked downhill, they grew thicker until the slope looked like it was covered in them. At the bottom, he reached a quiet stream winding through the woods toward the lake. The soft murmur of water was the first real sound he'd heard, besides the scream of that bird.

Now another sound broke the silence—a rough, human voice shouting words he couldn't quite understand. He followed the sound and soon saw a strange figure sitting on the grass. The man was large and round, with a long, drooping nose and a reddish face that almost glowed like polished copper. He wore a dark green velvet coat with gold lace, a faded red vest, and silk stockings pulled up over his thick legs. His shoes were wide and buckled, and he wore a powdered white wig that reached his shoulders. In each hand, he held a dice box and seemed to be playing a game against himself, shouting out the results in a deep, croaky voice.

The old man lifted his dark eyes and called out, "Come sit down, Sir Bale!" He shook one of the dice boxes and pointed at a spot on the grass across from him.

Sir Bale knew right away—this had to be the strange man, the fortune-teller, or whatever he was, that Feltram had talked about. Feeling both nervous and curious, Bale walked over. He was ready to do whatever the man asked and wasn't going to risk upsetting him this time.

He sat where the man told him and took the dice box he offered. They began playing turn by turn, rolling three dice. The old man explained the game as they went, mixing in curses and shouts. When he didn't like a roll, his face twisted with anger so fierce that Sir Bale half-expected him to pull out a weapon and attack.

They played for a while, tossing gold coins back and forth across the grass like chips in a gambling hall. Then the old man suddenly shouted over his shoulder, "Drink!" and picked up a tall, cone-shaped glass that Sir Bale hadn't noticed before. He handed it to him, then picked up one for himself.

At that moment, a very tall, skinny man walked over. He wore a white uniform, had powdered hair, and a pale face that ended in a long, hooked nose. In each hand, he held a flask. When Sir Bale looked at the strange pair—the large man in green and red, and the thin one all in white—he was struck by how much they reminded him of the giant macaw and the sleek kite he'd seen earlier. It wasn't just the colors, but something about their posture and expressions too.

Without waiting for permission, the fat old man held up his glass. The pale servant poured from one of the flasks, filling it, then did the same for Sir Bale.

It was a tall glass, probably holding about half a pint, and the drink inside was strange but beautiful. The liquid shimmered like an opal, with purple and gold rings rippling out from the middle and back in from the edges, crossing over each other like a glowing, moving pattern.

"To better luck next time," said the old man, raising his glass with a grin. He winked with one eye and squinted the other, giving Sir Bale a look like they shared a secret. "You know what I mean."

Sir Bale raised the glass to his lips. Wine? Whatever it was, he had never tasted anything so delicious. He drank every drop, then set the glass down on the grass. As he turned back to the old gambler, who was also setting down his glass, he noticed someone else nearby.

A young woman sat quietly on the grass. She had a graceful figure and wore a long black dress. A black hood covered her head, and a dark mask—like the ones used at costume balls—hid her face. But the bit of skin he could see—her pale chin and neck—was beautiful. The way she moved and carried herself made him sure she was lovely underneath the mask.

She was leaning gently against the old man in the green and gold coat. Her arm was wrapped around his shoulder, and her small, pale hand rested over it.

"Ah, my little Geaiette," the old man said in a raspy voice. "Looks like it's time for us to head home." Then he turned to Sir Bale. "Well now, Bale Mardykes, I've got no complaints about you today. You crossed the lake, you played fair, you drank like a proper guest. Now we understand each other. This is the beginning of a bond that'll last. I'll let you go—for now. But when I call, you'll return."

Then he leaned toward the girl in black. "Whisper it to me, sweetheart, and I'll tell him the name of the winner at next month's Rindermere race."

She leaned close and whispered softly into his ear.

"That's right!" the old man shouted, grinding his teeth. "The winning horse will be Rainbow. Now get moving—fast—or I'll let loose my black dogs! Ho, ho, ho! They might just chase you down."

He yelled this with such wild anger, his face twisted, and his fist shaking, that Sir Bale didn't wait. He quickly tipped his hat in goodbye and turned to leave.

But then the same rough voice shouted after him, "You'll want that, you fool! Pick it up!"

A heavy object flew past him and landed with a thump. It was a large leather bag, old and stained, clearly packed with something heavy. It bounced once and rolled to a stop right in front of his feet.

He picked it up—it was indeed heavy.

He turned around to say thank you, but the strange pair was already walking away. The bulky man in green was limping and staggering along surprisingly fast, while the masked woman in black floated silently beside him into the shadows of the forest.

Sir Bale felt a chill run down his spine. He was alone again.

Holding the heavy bag tightly, he made his way back the way he had come. After about an hour of walking, he reached the place where he had first entered the woods. Passing the Druid stone and the towering oak, he looked down the glen and saw Philip Feltram standing by the lake's edge, right next to the boat, waiting for him.

Chapter XXI.
Rindermere

Feltram looked tense and upset when Sir Bale reached him. He was standing on the flat stone where the boat was tied.

"You found him?" Feltram asked.

"I did," said Sir Bale.

"The woman in black—was she there?"

"Yes, she was."

"And did you play the game with him?"

"I did."

"And what's that in your hand?"

"A bag. I think it's money—it's heavy. He threw it after me. We'll check it soon. Let's just get away from here first."

"He gave you some of his wine to drink?" Feltram asked, watching him closely. There was a strange glint in his eyes, like he was almost laughing.

"Yes, of course I drank it. I was trying to stay on his good side."

"Naturally."

The soft breeze that had carried them across the lake earlier had completely died down by now. The wind was gone, and the sun was already starting to set.

"Hand me an oar," said Sir Bale. "We can row back in just over an hour. I just want to leave this place."

He climbed into the boat, sat down, and placed the heavy leather bag at his feet. Then he took an oar. Feltram untied the rope and pushed the boat off from the shore. He sat down and began rowing with Sir Bale. Neither of them spoke for the first ten minutes, as the boat moved farther and farther from Cloostedd.

The leather bag was too big and bulky to hide, and Feltram clearly already knew about it, so Sir Bale didn't bother trying. The bag was old and dirty, tied at the top with a long leather strap. Bits of red wax still clung to it, as if it had been sealed once.

Sir Bale opened it—and found it packed with gold coins.

"Stop!" he said excitedly. "It's gold—real gold! And a lot of it, too!"

Feltram didn't react at all. He sat quietly, resting his elbow on his knee, looking far off like his thoughts were somewhere else.

Sir Bale couldn't wait any longer. He started counting the coins right there on the bench. When he was done, he had counted two thousand guineas.

It took a while, but once he'd stuffed all the coins back into the bag and tied it shut again, Feltram suddenly straightened up and snapped,

"Come on, grab your oar—unless you feel like drifting here all night. Look, the wind's starting to pick up from Golden Friars!"

Feltram glanced nervously toward Mardykes Hall and Snakes Island. Then he grabbed his oar and told Sir Bale to grab his, too. The Baronet didn't hesitate.

Rowing was slow and tiring—the boat wasn't built to go fast. By the time they were halfway across the lake, the sun had set, and the soft, gloomy colors of evening spread across the water and hills.

"Here comes the breeze—from Golden Friars," said Feltram. "It'll be enough to fill the sails now. If you're not afraid of ghosts or Snakes Island, we're lucky the wind's coming from that direction. If it came from Mardykes, we'd have a tough time rowing this old tub home."

He spoke like he was talking to himself and chuckled quietly as he adjusted the sail and took the tiller. The wind pushed them gently, and the boat drifted slowly toward Mardykes Hall in the distance.

The moon rose. Mist began to float over the lake, and the tall hills looked like ghostly giants in the pale light. Sir Bale leaned against the side of the boat, listening to the soft splashes of the water and thinking about everything that had happened. It all felt like a strange dream—except for the heavy bag of gold at his feet.

As they passed Snakes Island, a small patch of mist floated beside the boat. Sir Bale thought the boat tilted slightly whenever the mist came close, like something was pulling it. Each time, Feltram waved his hand toward the fog, and it would drift away—but it kept coming back, and Feltram kept repeating the motion.

Three weeks later, Sir Bale sat up in bed, looking pale and weak. His silk nightcap drooped to one side, and his thin hand lay still on the blanket where the doctor had just checked his pulse. The room was dim. He told Doctor Torvey everything that had happened that day.

"My dear sir," the doctor said with a laugh, "do you really believe all of that was real? Sounds more like fever dreams."

"I can't help believing it," said Sir Bale. "It feels as real to me as anything else I've lived through. Except that it's stranger, I have no reason to think it wasn't real."

"Come now," said the doctor. "That kind of thing is very common. People often start hallucinating before they even know they're sick."

"But what about the bag of gold?"

"Someone must have lent it to you. Ask Feltram when you're better. He seemed to know all about it when I spoke to him, and he didn't act like it was anything out of the ordinary. Just like that fisherman's tale—about the hand pulling Feltram into the water the night he nearly drowned. Anyone can see that was just the reflection of his own hand in the lightning. Once you're feeling stronger, I'm sure these dreams will fade."

"Maybe so," said Sir Bale.

Of course, Sir Bale didn't tell the doctor everything. He only shared parts of what happened at Cloostedd, made it seem like a weird accident, and claimed the old man had tossed him a bag with five guineas. He didn't say anything about the upcoming race.

So, Dr. Torvey told people that the fever had left Sir Bale with a few odd memories—nothing serious.

But those memories, real or not, stayed sharp in Sir Bale's mind even after he got better.

He made up his mind to go to the Rindermere races. With the leather purse still in hand, he planned to bet everything on Rainbow—the horse the strange man had said would win. He was glad to hear the odds were high against Rainbow, which meant a big win if the horse came through.

And that's exactly what happened. One horse was withdrawn, another ran off track, a third jockey was underweight, and a fourth hit the wrong post and got disqualified. In the end, Rainbow crossed the finish line first. Sir Bale won more money than he cared to say—enough to pay off a big debt and fix his finances.

After that, his luck only got better. He never went back to Cloostedd, but Feltram still visited the forest often, and people believed he brought back tips for Sir Bale's bets. Whatever the truth was, Sir Bale's luck never ran out. His debts vanished, and he no longer dreamed of living abroad. He stayed at Mardykes Hall, spent money fixing it up, and though he never crossed the lake again, he seemed to enjoy the view.

In other ways, he didn't change. He still lived a strange, quiet life. He saw no one at Mardykes and stayed private. The neighbors disliked him. They thought he was rude and sharp-tongued, and they kept their distance.

Rumors spread. People said his relationship with Feltram had flipped—now Sir Bale acted timid, and Feltram seemed to be in charge. Others claimed that Mrs. Julaper once told the Vicar's wife, in a hushed voice, that Sir Bale wasn't happier with his new wealth. She said he was moody and afraid of Feltram, and everyone in the house felt the same way. She even said he might be mad—or worse—and that she was ready to leave.

The Vicar's wife told Mrs. Torvey, and soon all of Golden Friars knew the story—and added a few details of their own.

Everyone started whispering that Sir Bale's racing success was tied to something strange in Cloostedd Forest. When Feltram heard the stories—especially the one about a ghost giving Sir Bale a bag of gold—he laughed.

"You really shouldn't talk to Dr. Torvey like that," he said with a grim smile. "He's the worst gossip in town. That money came from old Farmer Trebeck. He's rich enough to buy us all. He lent me the money—not just out of kindness, but I gave him a signed note, and you signed a bond for those two thousand guineas. Funny you don't remember talking with that nice old man for so long. His grandson trains horses for Lord Varney and sometimes shares betting tips. That's where your lucky guesses really come from."

"I must be going a little crazy, that's all," said Sir Bale with a smile and a shrug.

Philip Feltram wandered around the house looking gloomy, doing whatever he liked. The changes in him were becoming more obvious. He always looked dark and serious—sometimes even angry. It was as if he had one dark thought stuck in his head all the time.

People whispered old superstitions about him and Sir Bale—saying maybe the Baronet had made some deal with the devil. Of course, no one said it out loud, especially since Sir Bale still had influence in town. But the rumor was really just an exaggerated version of what people secretly suspected in earlier, more superstitious times.

One evening at dusk, Sir Bale was sitting by his window after dinner. He spotted Feltram standing still by the lake, tall and stiff like a shadow. The sight made him feel uneasy and annoyed. He poured himself two glasses of brandy for courage and went down to the water's edge to stand next to him.

"Looking out my window," said Sir Bale, now feeling bolder from the drink, "and seeing you standing there like a statue—do you know what popped into my head?"

Feltram turned to look at him but didn't reply.

"I started thinking maybe I should get married."

Feltram gave a small nod. The news didn't seem to interest him at all.

"Why do you always have to act like this—so gloomy? Can't you just be like you used to be? I won't live here with you alone like this anymore. I'll take a wife, I swear it. A proper, churchgoing woman— she'll have the whole house praying on their knees twice a day, and three times on Sunday. What do you think about that?"

"Yes, you'll marry," said Feltram calmly, as if he already knew it would happen. His steady voice made Sir Bale feel a little cold inside, because he hadn't actually decided yet.

Then Feltram quietly walked away, and that was the end of their strange conversation.

Around that same time, something unusual happened. There was another branch of the Feltram family living near Carlisle. Records showed they were distant cousins of the Feltrams of Cloostedd. The family had three daughters, all known for their beauty.

One had married Sir Oliver Haworth, a powerful man who had even turned down a baronet title and was said to be hoping for a peerage. Another had married Sir William Walsingham, another wealthy baronet. The youngest, Miss Janet, was still single and living at Cloudesly Hall with her aunt, Lady Harbottle, who served as her chaperone.

As it happened, Sir Bale had business in Carlisle and, since he knew Lady Harbottle, stopped by Cloudesly Hall. Although he was already forty-five and had always thought himself too jaded for love, he fell seriously for Janet.

Janet was very pretty, with fair skin, bright red lips, large blue eyes, and dimples that showed when she smiled. It might seem strange, but even a man as cold and distant as Sir Bale could fall under her spell.

What was even stranger was that Janet fell for him too—deeply. No one could understand why. Her family tried to stop her. Her friends warned her. Even her old nurse begged her not to go through with it. But nothing worked. Oddly enough, Sir Bale didn't even try to win her over. Still, they ended up married, and she came to live at Mardykes Hall, determined to make everyone happy and be the happiest woman in England.

She brought along a cousin, Gertrude Mainyard, who was much older—over thirty—and looked pale and sad, but was gentle and still quite attractive for her age.

Gertrude had her own quiet love story. Her sweetheart was far away in India, and she was patiently waiting for him to return. All her hopes were tied to that uncertain reunion, and she lived quietly, holding onto that dream.

When Lady Mardykes arrived at the Hall, things seemed to take a turn for the better. Neighbors were ready to give the place another chance. People visited, and Lady Mardykes was well-liked and admired. She was charming—it was hard not to like her.

But that's where the friendliness ended. Sir Bale kept avoiding the kinds of dinners and parties that build real friendships. Some thought he was jealous of his young, beautiful wife. Most people just said he was the same as always—cold and unfriendly—and before long, the Hall's driveway was quiet again.

Sir Bale actually enjoyed this quiet life, and his wife—so in love with him, according to the other young women—didn't seem to mind. She was happy to skip the company of others just to spend more time with her husband. People couldn't understand what she saw in him or how she could stand being so isolated.

More than a year passed like this. Lady Mardykes was still happy—very happy, except for one thing: she and her husband could never agree when it came to Philip Feltram. And that turned into one very strange disagreement.

Chapter XXII.

Sir Bale is Frightened

Lady Mardykes felt a strong fear of Philip Feltram the moment she met him. It wasn't just that she didn't like him—she was truly afraid. Even though she didn't see him often, her fear kept growing. Eventually, she begged Sir Bale to let him go. She even offered to give Feltram a generous yearly payment from her own money if that's what it took.

There had been a time when Sir Bale also wanted Feltram gone. But that had changed. Now, no matter what she said, he refused to send him away. At first, he brushed off her requests calmly. But she kept pushing, and when she wouldn't let it go, he finally snapped. He got so angry that he threatened to leave her and the country altogether if she mentioned it again.

His sudden outburst shocked her. Until that moment, he had always been kind and loving. The argument left her in tears, frightened and upset. She stayed in her room for several days, and shortly after, Sir Bale left for London and didn't return for over a week. That was the first real trouble in their marriage.

The issue was dropped after that, but not long after he came home, something happened that brought all those same fears back.

Sir Bale had a small room away from the bedrooms where he would read or smoke. One night, when the whole house was quiet, a loud, frantic ringing came from that room. It sounded like someone in serious danger was yanking the bell rope in panic.

Lady Mardykes, still awake with her maid, heard it and rushed out in her dressing gown. When she reached the hallway, the butler Mallard was already trying to break down the locked door. It gave way just as she arrived.

Inside, Sir Bale stood holding the bell cord, pale and shaken like he'd seen something terrifying. Sitting calmly in a chair nearby was Feltram, staring at him with a cold, eerie smile.

For a moment, Lady Mardykes thought Feltram had tried to harm her husband. What else could explain such a frightening scene?

But Sir Bale held her as she cried and kept saying that nothing like that had happened.

Later, she told her cousin that she would never forget the look on Feltram's face that night.

Sir Bale never explained what had actually happened in that room. All she knew was that Feltram had come to tell him he'd be leaving within the year.

"You're probably happy to hear that," Sir Bale said. "But if you knew everything, maybe you wouldn't be. Whatever curse is flying around will land right where it came from. So let's stop talking about him. You got your wish—dis iratis."

That night seemed to mark a turning point between the two men. Afterward, they barely spoke. And when they did, their words were cold and distant, like they hardly knew each other.

One day, Sir Bale saw Feltram standing by the lake. He walked over and said quietly,

"I've been thinking… if I really do owe that money to old Trebeck, I should pay him. I was sick and not thinking clearly at the time, but I did benefit from it. I'd rather not have that debt show up again with interest added later."

"The old man meant it as a gift," Feltram replied. "He's richer than you are. He wanted to help the family. I think he burned the paperwork. He won't take your money."

"No one should force their money on someone else," said Sir Bale. "I never asked for it. And honestly, the whole thing still feels more like something I imagined than anything real. But you say it happened."

"People are responsible for what they mean to do—and what they think they've done," said Feltram, his voice sharp.

"So I'm responsible for what I imagined was a creepy old gambler?" Sir Bale replied. "Fine. But I still want to pay Trebeck back. Can you set it up?"

Feltram nodded toward the water. "Look over there. Trebeck just landed. He's staying at the George and Dragon tonight—he's here to sell cattle at the Golden Friars fair tomorrow. You can speak to him yourself."

And with that, Feltram quietly walked away, leaving Sir Bale alone to deal with the wealthy farmer.

A wide flight of steps led from the courtyard down to the jetty by the lake. Sir Bale walked down and approached the elderly farmer, Trebeck. He was cheerful, honest, and spoke in a thick local accent that was hard for anyone else to understand.

Sir Bale invited him to the Hall for lunch, but Trebeck said he couldn't stay. His cattle had arrived, and a pony was waiting nearby to take him to Golden Friars. He had to be on his way.

Then Sir Bale gently placed a hand on his arm, trying to sound both respectful and sincere, and quietly brought up the real reason he wanted to talk.

The old farmer stared at him for a moment, then laughed loudly—a kind of laugh that would've been too much indoors—and said, "I don't have any bond of yours, man."

"I know that," said Sir Bale. "So does Philip Feltram."

"Well?"

"Well, I still want to repay the money."

Trebeck laughed again and, in his heavy accent, told Sir Bale to wait until he actually asked for it. Sir Bale kept trying to insist, but the old man only answered with more teasing and laughter. The more annoyed Sir Bale got, the funnier the farmer seemed to find it. Finally, Trebeck climbed onto his shaggy pony and rode off, still chuckling, toward Golden Friars.

When he arrived at the George and Dragon Inn, he joked with Richard Turnbull, asking if he'd ever heard of someone turning down money, or of someone trying to repay money they didn't owe. He even wondered aloud if the Squire down at Mardykes Hall might not be "a little touched in the head." Still, many believed the truth was that Trebeck had quietly given the money as a gift, out of loyalty to the old family, and simply didn't want any credit or repayment. Some believed this, others didn't—opinions were divided.

Meanwhile, Feltram began to change in a strange way. Like a caterpillar right before it turns into something else, his moods grew darker. He barely spoke. He seemed constantly angry and full of restless energy. He spent hours walking alone in the woods above Mardykes, mumbling to himself, picking up dead branches, snapping them, throwing them aside, and stomping the ground as he paced back and forth.

One night, a thunderstorm rolled in. The wind was blowing gently from Golden Friars, and the sky was pitch black, lit now and then by flashes of lightning. At the bottom of the stairs, Sir Bale ran into Feltram, whom he hadn't seen for a few days. Feltram was wearing a cloak and hat.

"I'm going to Cloostedd tonight," he said. "And if things turn out the way I think they will, I won't be coming back. You and I both know what happened." He gave a single nod and walked off down the hallway.

Sir Bale immediately felt something had changed forever. He felt weak and sick and returned to his room. He didn't go to bed at all that gloomy night.

The next morning, he learned that a man named Marlin had seen Feltram late at night pushing the boat into the lake and sailing across. It had been too dark to see more than that, but with the light wind behind him, Feltram could've made it to the other side easily, without needing to turn or adjust course.

Feltram never came back. The boat was later found tied up at the Cloostedd landing.

Lady Mardykes was relieved. For a while, she was happier than ever. But it wasn't the same for Sir Bale—and before long, her happiness began to fade too.

Chapter XXIII.
A Lady in Black

Not long after, a stranger arrived at the George and Dragon inn. He looked a little over forty, with skin darkened by years of travel. For his age, he was surprisingly handsome. His eyes were warm, his dark brown hair had no gray, and when he smiled, his teeth were bright and even. He asked a lot of questions about the people nearby—especially about Mardykes Hall. He seemed very interested in what he heard. When he asked about Philip Feltram and learned that he was no longer living at the Hall and that neither Trebeck nor anyone else knew where he'd gone, the man started to cry.

He asked the innkeeper, Richard Turnbull, to take him to a quiet room. As they walked, the man gave Turnbull a kind smile, shook his hand, and said,

"Mr. Turnbull, don't you remember me?"

Turnbull looked puzzled. "No, sir. I can't say I do."

The stranger gave a soft, sad smile and shook his head. Still holding Turnbull's hand, he laughed gently and said, "I would've known you anywhere—whether on land or sea. If I'd seen you on a mountain in India, or floating on a boat in China, or even walking into a mosque in Turkey, I would've known you. Of course, I've changed a lot. You were always a little older than me, and you haven't changed nearly as much. I used to play handball in the yard here at the George. You'd bet a pint of ale on me. You always said I'd be the best handball player and singer for miles around. You even let me work behind the bar when I was just a hungry kid. I was staying at Mardykes Hall then, and I used to ride back in old Marlin's boat. Is Marlin still around?"

"He is," said Turnbull slowly, studying him more closely. "I can't think who you'd be—unless... unless you're that boy—William Feltram. But he was a good bit younger than Philip. No, that can't be."

"Yes, Mr. Turnbull. I'm that boy—Willie Feltram. It's really me. Come on, shake my hand like an old friend."

Turnbull grinned wide and shook his hand hard. "That I will!" he said, laughing. William's eyes filled with tears.

Later, after they had talked a while in private, William asked, "Now that we can talk honestly, can you please tell me what happened to my brother Philip? A friend told me something about his health that's been worrying me terribly."

"Philip was strong," said Turnbull. "He loved to hike the hills and row across the lake. But people started saying his mind wasn't right anymore. They said something about Mardykes Hall seemed to affect him. But that's a longer story."

"Yes," said William quietly. "That's what I was told too—that he wasn't himself anymore. I've been so anxious ever since. If I just knew he was safe, I'd be happy. Where is he now?"

"One night, he crossed the lake after saying goodbye to Sir Bale. Everyone thought he was headed to visit old Trebeck up in the hills. Trebeck always liked the Feltrams, even though the families weren't always on good terms. But Trebeck never saw him, and no one else has either. No one knows what happened to him."

"I heard that too," William said with a heavy sigh. "But I was hoping the mystery would've been solved by now. I'd give almost anything just to know what became of him. I just want peace."

He paused and added, "Now, my good old friend, please have someone get a carriage ready. I need to go to Mardykes Hall. But first, could you give me a room so I can change?"

At Mardykes Hall, a pale and beautiful woman stood by the window, staring out into the quiet courtyard. She looked beyond the stone railing and the large flowerpots, their leaves scattered and blown away by the wind—just like her hopes. The tall, misty hills and the gentle ripple of the lake made her feel even more alone.

Then she heard the rare sound of a carriage approaching.

Before it even stopped, the door flew open and William Feltram jumped out.

Somehow, she was already in the hall—she didn't even remember running there—and with a loud cry and a sob, she threw herself into his arms.

Finally, the long wait was over—the sadness and hopelessness were gone. Like two people saved after a shipwreck, they hugged each other tightly, full of joy.

William didn't return with a huge fortune, but he had just enough to get married. Most people might have thought it wasn't enough. But he was back home, healthy and stronger after everything he'd gone through overseas. He believed he could find a way to earn more, and he was sure that even a small income would bring them more happiness than lots of money ever could.

It had been five years since he and Gertrude had said goodbye in France, where his work in India had taken him on a business trip.

William had always loved art, music, and culture. Those interests caught the attention of Lady Harbottle and her traveling group. When Miss Janet—who later became Lady Mardykes—found out his last name was Feltram, she asked a friend about him and became even more curious. That led to an introduction, and William's kind, gentle personality quickly turned that meeting into a close friendship.

He had always been proud and wanted to succeed on his own. He'd done well enough that he didn't need help. He hadn't heard directly from his brother, but a friend in London had kept him updated. More recently, Gertrude's letters had told him worrying things about Philip.

When Lady Mardykes saw William again, she was thrilled. She already had a plan for his and Gertrude's future. She wanted him to take over the large farm on the Mardykes estate—or if he preferred, manage it for her and share the profits. The idea excited her. The farm was close—just half a mile up the lake. The house was cozy, the garden lovely, and Gertrude would still be nearby. In fact, William and Gertrude could spend most of their time at the Hall if they wanted.

Lady Mardykes was so excited and persistent that William couldn't say no. As soon as they were married, the plan was set in motion. For a while, they were the happiest neighbors anyone could remember.

But even with all of that, was Lady Mardykes truly happy? Had she escaped the quiet sadness many people feel inside? Her biggest wish was to have children. Again and again, she was left heartbroken.

She had one sweet little baby who lived for two years before passing away. No other child ever came. The nursery stayed empty and silent. That kind of sadness is hard for others to understand.

Another pain came from her husband. Sir Bale Mardykes started to dislike William Feltram, and no one knew why. At first, he hid it, but over time, it became obvious. Eventually, he told his wife he wanted William to move away. He created small problems and annoyances until one day, he just said it outright.

Lady Mardykes begged him not to do it. She even cried. She knew if Gertrude left, her own life would feel empty and lonely.

Finally, Sir Bale gave her a reason. He told her there was an old story that said the Mardykes estate would one day belong to a Feltram. He said he had always felt uneasy about that family. He believed his instincts were a warning—that maybe someone was planning something. He even thought Trebeck might be involved. He reminded her that Philip Feltram once said Mardykes would go to a Feltram. Sir Bale said he wouldn't let that happen. He didn't want his wife to lose her inheritance or any children they might have to be left with nothing.

It all sounded a little crazy—but the idea had come from Philip Feltram. Deep down, Sir Bale's jealousy was tied to a superstition he didn't want to admit. He regretted ever letting William live on the estate.

Because of all this stress, William seriously thought about giving up the farm and starting over somewhere else.

One day, walking alone through the thick woods near his land, he kept asking himself, "Should I quit? Should I just return the lease if that's what he wants?"

All of a sudden, a voice shouted nearby:

"Hold it, you fool! Hold hard, you fool! Hold it, you fool!"

Startled and confused—he had thought he was alone—William looked around. Just then, a huge parrot with green, red, and yellow feathers dropped from the trees. It flapped, stumbled, and hopped along the ground before vanishing into the underbrush. William never saw it again.

It reminded him of a scene from Robinson Crusoe. It was strange—and because he didn't own any bird like that, it felt like a sign. Something he was meant to notice.

When he got home, he told Gertrude about it. They were living quiet, often emotional lives, so she didn't laugh like she might have when she was feeling more cheerful.

They kept talking about whether they should move, especially since a similar farm just fifteen miles away was now available. Gertrude, who felt hurt by Sir Bale's coldness—especially since they had discovered they were distant cousins—strongly wanted to leave. She kept gently urging her husband to agree.

Then something strange happened that made her think twice.

She had gone to bed thinking about the move. Though she couldn't remember falling asleep, it felt like she was still awake. A candle burned beside her as she waited for William to return from a fair near Haworth. Everything in the room looked normal. It was a hot night, and the window was cracked open just a little. She heard a small sound coming from the window—and to her surprise, a jay bird hopped up onto the sill and came into the room.

Gertrude sat up quickly, surprised and a little shaken by the sudden appearance of such a large bird. For a moment, she was too stunned to even try to scare it away. She stared at it with wide eyes. A sofa stood at the foot of the bed, and the bird quickly hopped underneath it. Gertrude reached out to pull the bell rope on her left, which made the bed curtains shift. They had only been slightly open at the bottom.

She was shocked to see a woman standing there—dressed completely in black, with an old-style hood covering her head. The woman was young and pretty. She looked at Gertrude kindly, but now and then her lips and eyebrows twitched slightly, like she was in pain. These little movements came and went, about once or twice a minute.

Gertrude never understood later why she hadn't been more frightened. Something about the woman's presence—maybe the soft expression on her face—made her feel calm, despite how strange it was. The woman held a white handkerchief to her chest with a very pale hand.

"Who are you?" Gertrude asked.

"I'm a relative," the woman said. "Even though you don't know me. I've come to tell you that you must not leave Faxwell or Janet. If you try to go, I'll come with you—and I can make you fear me."

Her voice was quiet and faint, but strangely clear. It didn't sound like it came through Gertrude's ears, but rather straight into her head.

Then the woman gave a terrible smile and lifted her handkerchief. Beneath it was a deep wound in her chest, and inside the wound, Gertrude could see the dark head of a snake twisting.

Gertrude screamed and dove under the covers, frozen with terror. She stayed like that until her maid, alarmed by the scream, rushed in. At Gertrude's request, the maid searched the room and closed the window, trying her best to comfort her.

Whether it was a dream or just her imagination, shaped by all the worries she'd had lately, the vision left a strong impression. Whatever it was, it convinced her not to leave Faxwell. So the matter was settled—and the tension between the farm's tenants and the master of Mardykes Hall continued.

All of this was deeply upsetting to Lady Mardykes, even though Sir Bale never forced her to cut ties with her cousin. Still, Gertrude no longer came to Mardykes Hall. Even Lady Mardykes thought it was better to visit her at Faxwell rather than risk a fight with her husband. And so, the years passed.

No one ever heard any news about Philip Feltram. Nothing ever reached the area. If it hadn't seemed so unlikely that he could have drowned without his body ever being found, people would have assumed he had ended his life in the lake, either by accident or on purpose.

There was a gloomy feeling over Mardykes Hall. No children's voices filled the halls, and even the hope of having a child had faded.

This heartbreak likely added to Sir Bale's growing fear that his estate wasn't secure. He developed the strange belief that William Feltram and old Trebeck were secretly working together to take the property. Of course, this idea was completely irrational.

Still, in other ways, Sir Bale was sharp and smart—a quick thinker and a capable man in business. So while his suspicion seemed strange, it wasn't entirely shocking in someone naturally suspicious like him.

In the seven years since Sir Bale married Miss Janet Feltram, only two events had brought mourning to the house: the death of their only child, and the death of Sir William Walsingham, Lady Mardykes' brother-in-law. His widow now lived in a beautiful old house in Islington. She was wealthy and sometimes visited Mardykes Hall, often bringing Lady Haworth, their other sister. Sir Oliver, Lady Haworth's husband, spent most of his time in London with Parliament, busy with politics—and, like many social gentlemen, sometimes struggling with gout.

Despite the time apart, the sisters stayed very close. No three sisters could have been more loving.

Was Lady Mardykes happy in her marriage? For a woman as kind and gentle as she was, happiness didn't require much—just a husband who wasn't cruel. There must have been something good in Sir Bale, because his wife clearly loved him deeply. She admired his intelligence, respected his strong will, and in many ways worshipped him at home. That kind of devotion doesn't come from nothing—there had to be something likable about him. In fact, what others saw as blind devotion only seemed to grow stronger over time.

Chapter XXIV.
An Old Portrait

Sir Bale, once remembered as a cheerful and social man—though some called him reckless—had now become quiet and gloomy. It was clear that something was weighing on his mind. Some people in Golden Friars even whispered that maybe, if there were any evidence, they might believe he had killed Philip Feltram and was now haunted by guilt.

His dark mood spread through the house. Even the servants seemed low-spirited, and the house felt cold and haunted, like it had seen something terrible.

Lady Mardykes had a love for art. One day, she discovered a bunch of old portraits in a forgotten room. Some were full-length paintings. With the help of her maid, both wearing aprons and surrounded by basins, cloths, and brushes, she worked to clean them up. As they removed layers of dust and soot, the colors and fine details slowly came back to life.

When Sir Bale walked into the room, Lady Mardykes was in the middle of restoring one of the paintings.

"Oh!" she said, turning to him with a smile, a brush in her hand. "We're in a mess! Munnings and I have been cleaning these old pictures. Mrs. Julaper said they came from Cloostedd Hall long ago. They were stuffed away in the dark room in the clock tower. Look at this one! I think it's from the time of King George I or II. The colors are so bold, and his face is so lifelike—it feels like he's about to speak!"

Sir Bale stepped closer and looked over her shoulder at the painting. As he did, his expression changed in a strange way.

The portrait showed a man with a dark, unhealthy face, like he drank too much. He had small, mean-looking eyes, a sagging nose, and a grim mouth. A large wart sat just above his lips. He wore one of those big powdered wigs that looked like a fluffy cloud. His outfit included a lace cravat, black velvet breeches with rolled-down stockings, a dark green velvet coat, and a deep red waistcoat trimmed with gold. He had a sword and leaned on a cane, clearly swollen with gout and age— probably about sixty. The painting was powerful, and the man in it looked angry and harsh.

Lady Mardykes laughed softly. "What wild outfits they wore! He looks like something out of a magical lantern show. The colors are like a parrot's feathers. Look at his claw-like hand and that huge broken nose! Doesn't he look like a mean old parrot?"

"Where did you find that?" Sir Bale asked.

She was surprised by his tone and even more by the way he looked at the picture.

"I told you, in the clock tower," she said gently. "I hope it wasn't wrong to bring them here. Are you upset, Bale?"

"Upset? No," he said, "I just wish it was in the fire. I must have seen that picture as a child. I hate looking at it. I even had nightmares about it once when I was sick. I don't know who it is, and I don't want to. Please, have it burned."

"It's one of the Feltrams," she said. "'Sir Hugh Feltram' is written on the frame. Mrs. Julaper said he was the father of the woman who drowned near Snakes Island."

"So what?" he said. "That doesn't make it interesting. It's a horrible painting. I link it to my illness—and I believe just staring at it long enough could drive someone mad. Burn it. Let's leave this room. I can't think straight in here."

The longer he stayed, the more upset he got. He looked both frightened and angry, and he grabbed her wrist—not roughly, but urgently—and led her out of the room.

Once they were alone in a different room, he asked her again who had told her about the portrait and why she had cleaned it. She said the truth—it was a total accident. She had found it while exploring.

"If I thought you were planning something with others," he said, "talking behind my back and trying clever tricks—" He stopped, staring at her suspiciously.

She didn't say a word. She just looked at him with tearful eyes.

He let go of her wrist and gently touched her shoulder.

"Don't cry, Janet," he said. "I didn't mean to upset you. I only wanted to know if, by any chance, you've seen Philip Feltram. He might be behind all this. No one knows him like I do. Now, don't cry anymore. Just tell me honestly—has he come back? Is he at Faxwell?"

She told him no—and it was the truth. After a pause, he let it go. Once they both calmed down, he had something else to tell her.

"Sit down, Janet," he said more softly. "Forget that awful picture and everything I just said. What I came to tell you will make you happy—I know it will."

He put his arm around her and kissed her gently. She smiled through her tears. After he finished speaking, she threw her arms around him and kissed him in return, over and over, thanking him with all her heart.

It wasn't anything huge—but coming from Sir Bale, it was unexpected.

Was it just a sudden change of mood? Who knows? But early in that cold and serious month of December, Sir Bale told his wife that he wanted to invite some guests from the county to stay for a week or so near Christmas. He wanted her sisters—Lady Haworth and the Dowager Lady Walsingham—to come early so she could enjoy their company before the rest of the guests arrived.

Lady Mardykes was thrilled. She quickly wrote to her sisters, asking them to arrive around the 10th or 12th of December. They agreed.

Sir Oliver, Lady Haworth's husband, couldn't make it. A government minister was staying in Bath for his health, and Sir Oliver thought it wouldn't hurt to go drink the healing waters too. His doctor agreed, so off he went. He was sorry to miss Christmas with that "jolly fellow Bale" at Mardykes, but health came first—even if he ended up drinking more wine than water in Bath.

So, around December 8th, Lady Walsingham and Lady Haworth set off in a fine carriage from the Dower House in Islington, along with all their usual servants. They planned to take four days for the journey, stopping at inns where rooms had been reserved in advance.

Lady Haworth hadn't been feeling well lately—tired and anxious. But the cold, sunny weather and the excitement of the trip lifted her spirits. She expected nothing but joy and celebration. After all, Sir Bale would just be one of many guests, and even he could be pleasant and charming when he wanted to. So they set off, full of hope, heading north toward Mardykes Hall.

Chapter XXV.
Through the Wall

On the third night of their journey, the sisters stayed at a warm and comfortable old inn called the Three Nuns. They could have made it to Mardykes Hall that same evening—it was only around thirty-five miles away. But Lady Walsingham, wanting to make sure her sister didn't get too tired, had planned the trip to go at a gentle pace with no long, exhausting days.

They took the best sitting room in the inn, and even though the journey had been tiring, Lady Haworth stayed up chatting cheerfully with her sister until nearly ten o'clock.

Lady Walsingham was the oldest of the three sisters. At home, she was used to taking the lead, and her younger sisters often relied on her for advice and decision-making. It wasn't something she demanded— it came naturally. They trusted her because she was confident, thoughtful, and calm.

Eventually, Lady Haworth, feeling more tired than her sister, said goodnight and headed to bed. The two women kissed each other goodnight warmly.

Lady Walsingham wasn't sleepy yet, so she stayed in the sitting room a little longer. She passed the time reading the same book that had helped her get through the quieter parts of the trip. Her sister had been in her room for almost an hour when Lady Walsingham began to feel a little drowsy herself. She lit her candle and was about to ring for her maid when something unexpected happened—the door opened, and her sister walked in wearing a dressing gown, looking pale and frightened.

"My dear Mary!" cried Lady Walsingham. "What's wrong? Are you feeling okay?"

"I think so," Mary said softly, "but I'm scared, Maud. I don't know why—I just feel afraid."

She paused, turning her eyes toward one of the walls, listening closely.

"Oh Maud, I'm really scared. I can't explain it."

"Try not to worry, love," Lady Walsingham said gently. "You were probably dreaming. Did you fall asleep?"

Mary clutched her sister's arm with both hands and stared into her face.

"Did you hear anything?" she whispered, still looking toward the wall like she expected to hear something again.

"Nonsense, Mary," said her sister, trying to calm her. "You're still shaken from a dream. I've been awake the whole time. If there had been a noise, I would've heard it. Now come sit down and drink a little water. You're just tired and nervous. Tell me exactly what scared you, because nothing at all has happened here. This is the quietest inn in England, and I can't read minds—so tell me what's going on."

Mary sat down slowly, her eyes still wide as she looked around the room. She hadn't even touched the glass of water in her hand.

"I don't hear it now. You don't either, do you?"

"Please," Lady Walsingham said gently but firmly, "just tell me what you're talking about."

Mary took a deep breath. "You were right—I had a dream, and I can barely remember most of it. But the end of it… that's what scared me. I was so tired when I got into bed, I thought I'd fall asleep right away—and I did. I must've slept for quite a while. How long ago did I leave you?"

"Over an hour," said Lady Walsingham.

"Yes, then I must've been asleep for a while. I've only been awake for about ten minutes. I don't remember the beginning of the dream, but near the end, it felt so real. I was standing in an alcove in a hallway with wooden walls—really tall, old-fashioned, and beautiful. I could see the top of a big staircase with a thick oak banister. Right near me, just about as far away as that window, was a short column of carved wood with a candle on top. That candle was the only light in the whole place."

"There was a woman standing by the candle. Her back was to me, and she was looking down the stairs, like she was talking to someone below. I couldn't see who she was speaking to, but I could tell from the way she moved that she was in a lot of pain. She kept pressing her hands to her chest, wringing them, and shaking her head like she was really upset."

"But I couldn't hear her. Not a single sound. Even when she hit the banister or stamped her foot, I couldn't hear anything. I was just standing there, watching her, feeling so sad for her. I didn't know who she was—until she turned around."

Mary stopped for a second, swallowing hard. "It was Janet. Her face was pale, covered in tears, and she looked heartbroken—like nothing I've ever seen. I'll never forget it."

"Oh Mary," said Lady Walsingham, wrapping an arm around her. "It was just a dream. That's all. I've had dozens worse. You're just extra sensitive right now. Don't let it worry you."

"But that's not even the worst part. What happened next was so frightening that I don't know if something terrible is going on at Mardykes—or if I'm just losing my mind," said Lady Haworth, her voice shaking more and more. "I woke up right away, really scared. But I told myself it was just like any other nightmare, and tried to calm down. I sat up in bed, thinking I'd call Winnefred because my heart was pounding. But then I felt a little better and decided not to.

"While I was sitting there, I heard a faint sound, like someone talking through a thick wall. It came from the wall to the left of my bed. I thought it sounded like a woman crying or begging in fear. It was too quiet to make out the words, but I could tell she was very upset. I listened carefully, wondering who it could be and what had happened. Then I heard my name. At first, I thought it might be a coincidence— there are plenty of people named Mary. But I was curious, and something strange happened. I was staring at that very wall and realized there was a window in it.

"I thought maybe there was still another room on the other side. So I pulled back the curtain and looked out. But there's no room—just the outside wall. The other walls can't be hiding rooms either. One wall has two windows, and the one behind my bed faces the hallway. I noticed that clearly earlier when I walked to your room."

"Come now, Mary dear," said Lady Walsingham gently. "Sounds can be so tricky—you'd be surprised how often your ears play tricks. That and your imagination can explain all of this."

"But I'm not done," Lady Haworth said. "The voice got louder, and then I could hear it clearly—it was Janet. She was calling out to both of us, begging us to come to Mardykes right away. She sounded desperate, as if she was losing her mind. She called you by name too, just as urgently. It was definitely her voice. It still sounded like it came through a wall, but I could understand every word. I've never heard anyone sound so heartbroken. She was pleading with us to come now—right now—or she'd go mad."

"Well, my love," said Lady Walsingham, trying to stay calm, "you said she called me too, so I suppose I'm included in this ghostly invitation. But I promise you, we'll laugh about this tomorrow with Janet herself once we reach Mardykes. What you really need is some rest and maybe a little sal-volatile."

She rang the bell for Lady Haworth's maid, helped her calm down, and made sure she took something to settle her nerves. Then she walked her to her room, sat in the armchair by the fire, and promised to stay until she fell asleep and was resting peacefully.

But Lady Haworth had only been in bed for about ten minutes when she suddenly sat up, her eyes wide and her lips parted as she listened hard.

"There it is again!" she cried in horror. "She's blaming us—don't you hear it? I can't stay here a second longer!"

She jumped out of bed and rang the bell loudly.

"Maud," she cried out, terrified, "nothing will keep me here. Whether you come with me or not, I'm leaving as soon as the horses are ready. If you stay, the responsibility is yours. Listen!" She pointed to the wall, her face pale and her eyes wide with fear. "Don't you hear her?"

Even Lady Walsingham, who had tried to stay calm, looked pale. Fear of the supernatural can be contagious. She still tried to say it was all in Mary's mind, but the panic had clearly gotten to her too.

"Alright, dear Mary," she said, "if you feel so strongly about it, there's no point in arguing. You can't sleep here in this state. Let's go to Mardykes—maybe you'll feel better once we're there."

Mary was already throwing on her clothes like someone running from danger. Lady Walsingham gave orders to get the horses ready and prepare for them to continue their journey.

It was now between ten and eleven at night. But their guard, who rode with them armed—as was common in those days—thought they could reach Mardykes Hall before three in the morning if they gave the postboys a little extra pay to hurry.

As the carriage rolled out, Lady Haworth felt a bit calmer. The ghostly voice was gone, but the fear and worry it caused still lingered.

Lady Walsingham tried to start a conversation but quickly fell quiet. A thin layer of snow covered the dark landscape, and a few flakes were still drifting down. She checked the time often in the dark and asked about the remaining distance repeatedly. Though she wasn't physically tired, she was eager to get there. Whatever had shaken her sister so deeply had now left her feeling anxious too.

Chapter XXVI.
Perplexed

Even back then, the roads were in good condition, and the inns had excellent horses. So, with some extra payment, the servant was able to keep up a fast pace for the first few parts of the journey.

As they got closer to Mardykes Hall, Lady Walsingham kept checking her watch, growing more anxious even though she tried not to show it. Her sister, Lady Haworth, wasn't as calm. Despite the cold and falling snow, she kept leaning out the carriage window, and when she sat back down, she would say aloud how worried she was and ask her sister for reassurance.

The village of Golden Friars looked strange and quiet under its thin layer of snow. Everyone had long since gone to bed, and the two women were tense as their carriage stopped in front of the George and Dragon inn. They rang the bell and knocked loudly until someone finally answered.

A few minutes later, the door opened, and the porter, still half-asleep, stumbled out after talking briefly to the driver. He came over to the carriage window.

"Is Lady Mardykes okay?" asked Lady Walsingham.

"What about Sir Bale?"

"Is everyone at Mardykes Hall alright?"

Lady Haworth sat still with her hands tightly clasped, listening closely as her sister asked the questions one after another. The porter answered each one—yes, everyone was fine. Lady Walsingham let out a relieved breath and gave her sister a small, reassuring smile as she gently squeezed her hand. Lady Haworth whispered, "Thank God," and tears began to fall.

"When did you last hear from the Hall?" Lady Walsingham asked.

"A servant was here around four o'clock," the man replied.

"No one since?" she asked, sounding disappointed.

"No, ma'am. But everything was fine then."

"They're early to bed at Mardykes," she said to her sister. "It's dark by four, and that's likely the last they'd have sent anyone out. Nothing could've happened since—not likely. It's just past two, and we came very fast."

Still, both women felt their anxiety creeping back.

While the staff at the inn hurried to get fresh horses ready, Lady Walsingham quietly told her servant—who knew the village well—to wake the people at Doctor Torvey's house and find out if anything had happened at Mardykes.

Her servant returned with news: the doctor had been called to the Hall around ten o'clock, but he hadn't come back yet. No one knew why he was needed, and there was no word of anyone being sick. While Lady Haworth chatted with her maid near one carriage window, Lady Walsingham received this news at the other, unnoticed. It made her feel uneasy.

A few minutes later, they were back on the road with fresh horses, racing toward the Hall.

About two miles out, the carriage suddenly stopped. A voice from the side of the road spoke—it was a servant from Mardykes, sent with a note for Lady Walsingham. If needed, he had been told to ride all the way to the Three Nuns to deliver it. Lady Walsingham already had the letter in her hands. Her sister sat beside her as she opened it and read quickly by the light of the carriage lamp the man held to the window:

My dearest—my beloved sister—both of you, please! For the love of God, don't wait another second. I'm so scared and shaken I can hardly think. I don't know how to explain—just please come right away. I'm barely making sense as I write this. I feel like I'll completely fall apart if you don't get here soon. Please don't let me down.

Your heartbroken,

JANET

The sisters looked at each other, pale and shaken. Lady Haworth squeezed her sister's hand.

"Where's the messenger?" Lady Walsingham asked.

A mounted servant came to the window.

"Is anyone sick at the Hall?" she asked.

"No, ma'am. Everyone's fine. Lady Mardykes, Sir Bale—no one's sick."

"But the doctor was called. Why?"

"I'm not sure, ma'am."

"You're certain—really think—no one is sick?"

"No one that I know of, ma'am."

"Is my sister, Lady Mardykes, still awake?"

"Yes, ma'am. Her maid is with her."

"And Sir Bale—he's completely fine?"

"Yes, ma'am. He's been going over papers tonight. He seemed perfectly well."

"Alright, thank you," she said. Then to her servant she added, "Tell the driver to go as fast as they can. I'll pay them well."

Within a minute, the carriage was racing down the road again, the horses moving faster than a regular trot—their hooves muffled on the thin layer of snow, now more like a gallop.

Soon, they were under towering trees, black against the snow like dark feathers. The moonlight reflected off the cold surface of the lake, and the shape of Snakes Island came into view—its bare trees standing in a gloomy group, as if watching Mardykes Hall from across the water.

The carriage sped through the gates and between the tall rows of trees, and finally the steaming horses stopped, panting and snorting in front of the steps at the Hall.

A light was shining in an upstairs window, and a soft glow came from the hallway inside. The door opened, and an elderly servant stepped out to lead the ladies into the house.

Chapter XXVII.
The Hour

They carefully stepped over the snow-covered steps and walked inside, where they saw their sister standing in the large, dimly lit hall. Her maid held a single candle, and another burned on the table, leaving most of the big room in shadow. The flickering light made the figures look dramatic, like something out of a painting. A strip of cold moonlight from the open door stretched across the floor like a pale sheet at their feet.

Lady Mardykes let out a shaky breath of relief and quickly hugged each of her sisters. She kissed them over and over, thanking them, calling them her "blessed sisters," and praising God for sending them just in time. She was overwhelmed with emotion.

Holding one sister's hand in each of hers, she led them into a large room. The candlelight faintly lit up the edges of old, tall picture frames on the walls and the dark shapes of the portraits hanging in them. Moonlight came in slanted through the stone-framed windows and shimmered on the floor. The maid placed the candle on the sideboard, and Lady Mardykes told her she could leave.

"They don't know anything," she whispered. "They just think something strange is going on here—but they don't know the truth. God help me, not the truth. Sit down, my darlings. You must be tired."

She sat between them on the sofa, still holding their hands. They sat facing the window, where they could see the breathtaking view from the front of the house. In the foreground stood the dark trees of Snakes Island. One long branch stretched upward, still and bare, like an arm reaching toward the sky in warning or awe. Part of the lake shone with icy moonlight, glittering and trembling, while the rest disappeared into darkness. The snowy hills rose up beyond it, pale and sharp against the sky. The view stretched all the way to the shadowy woods of Cloostedd, the old land of the Feltrams.

Still wrapped in their cloaks and scarves, the sisters sat quietly, holding her hands, and listened closely as she began to tell her story.

Here's what she told them: About ten days ago—around the time Sir Bale had told her to invite their friends—he suddenly seemed lighter, like a burden had been lifted from him. That morning, he had gone for a walk with Trevor, the under-steward, to talk about thinning out some trees on the estate. They also planned to talk about a recent offer from a wealthy businessman who wanted to lease the old park and hunting grounds at Cloostedd for many years. The man hoped to build a new house there and restore the property.

Sir Bale had taken a strong interest in this idea. He even agreed to cross the lake with Trevor and walk the land, something he hadn't done in years because of his fear of water.

That morning, he had seemed happier than usual. He was full of energy and enthusiasm—more like a young man who had just inherited his land for the first time than the gloomy, nervous Baronet who had spent years pacing the halls of Mardykes, avoiding the lake like it was cursed.

As they were heading back to the boat, near the same old dead tree whose bare branch had once looked to Sir Bale like a skeleton's arm beckoning him into the woods, he and his companion suddenly realized they had lost the old map of the grounds they had been using.

"We must've left it in the tower room at Cloostedd House—the one where you can see the whole property," said the steward. "We really can't afford to lose it. It's the best map we have."

"I'll wait here and rest while you go get it," Sir Bale replied.

The man was only gone for about twenty minutes. When he came back, he found that Sir Bale had moved. He was now walking back and forth in a small clearing a few hundred steps closer to the path that led to the boat. At first, the steward thought Sir Bale was just impatient. But he wasn't—he looked upset. His face was pale, and for the first time ever, he reached out and took his companion's arm.

"Let's go. Quickly," Sir Bale said. "There's something I forgot—I have to tell you at home."

He didn't say another word on the way back. He sat in the back of the boat, looking as miserable as a man being taken to prison. When they reached the Hall, he went straight to his library and sat there in silence for a long time, looking shocked and shaken.

Eventually, he seemed to make a decision. He started calmly going through papers, sorting some and burning others. When it was time for dinner, he sent word to Lady Mardykes that he wouldn't be joining her but would see her afterward.

"It was sometime between eight and nine," Lady Mardykes said, "I can't remember exactly, when he came into the drawing room in the tower where I was sitting. I didn't hear him coming—there's a thick carpet on the stairs. He said he wanted to talk to me there. It's a quiet, out-of-the-way room, with very thick walls and two doors, one of solid oak. I think he chose it so no one could hear us."

She paused, clearly emotional. "He had a look on his face that frightened me. I could tell he had something terrible to say. He looked like someone who had been told he must carry out a death sentence. Oh, my poor Bale—my husband! He knew what this would mean to me."

Lady Mardykes began sobbing and couldn't speak for a while.

Then she continued, "He was calm and kind. He didn't say much, and I think these were his words: 'Janet, I've made a mistake. I thought my danger was over. We've had many years together, but a goodbye has to come eventually. My time has arrived.'"

"I don't even remember what I said back. I could hardly believe it—until I looked at him. But there was something in his voice and face that no one could question."

"'I'll be dead before morning,' he told me. 'You must be strong, Janet. There's no changing it now.'"

"I cried, 'Oh, Bale, you're not thinking of taking your own life!'"

"'No, poor girl,' he said, 'not that. I'm just going to die. No violence—just the way life fades away for everyone eventually. I've come to terms with it. It happens to millions of people every year, many worse than me. Don't come with me to my room. I'll see you again before it happens.'"

"His words were calm—cold, even. But his face looked like stone. I've never seen a face like that, not even in a dream."

Lady Walsingham tried to comfort her. "I'm sure he's just sick. He must have a fever. Don't torture yourself by believing these things. You sent for Doctor Torvey—what did he say?"

"I couldn't tell the doctor everything," said Lady Mardykes.

"Of course not," said her sister. "They'd just say he's lost his mind, and we're being silly for listening. But did the doctor see him? What did he say?"

"Yes, he saw him. He said there's nothing wrong—no fever, no illness of any kind. Bale only let him come to please me," she said through tears. "I begged him—it was my last hope. But there's no illness. Just wait until you see him. He's too calm, too clear. He knows exactly what he's doing. There's something terrifying about that."

Lady Mardykes broke down again, completely overcome with fear and grief.

Chapter XXVIII.
Sir Bale in the Gallery

Janet, you're just tired and worried, and you're letting Bale's fear scare you just as much as it scares him. The truth is, he's what doctors call a hypochondriac—he always thinks something's wrong with him. I'm sure I'm right. By morning, he'll feel better and probably be a little embarrassed about upsetting you like this. I'll stay up with you tonight. But Mary isn't that strong, and she really should lie down and get some rest. How about you make me a cup of tea in the drawing room? I'll go to my room quickly, change out of these clothes, and meet you there. Or, if you'd rather, you can sit with me in my room instead. Let's make it bright and cozy, with plenty of candles and a warm fire. And I promise, if you just use your usual good sense, you'll feel much calmer very soon.

Lady Walsingham spoke kindly and confidently. For a moment, Janet felt a bit of hope and admitted that maybe her sister was right. But fear spreads easily, and Lady Walsingham herself was starting to feel uneasy, though she kept it to herself.

She walked with Mary to her room, speaking to her just as encouragingly as she had with Janet. Then she went to her own room, took off her traveling clothes, and headed back downstairs. On the way, she heard Sir Bale's voice in the hallway, giving orders to a servant. He sounded exactly like himself.

Her heart jumped. She turned and saw him. He looked slightly more serious and pale than usual, but otherwise unchanged. He took her hand gently and held it, studying her face closely for a moment before motioning for the servant to go.

"I'm glad you came, Maud," he said. "You've heard what's going to happen. I don't think Janet could have handled it without you. You were right to come. Please stay with her for a few days—and take her away from here as soon as you can."

She looked at him, caught off guard and frightened. He spoke so calmly, like someone saying goodbye before something terrible.

"I'm glad to see you, Bale," she said, not sure what else to say, and stopped.

"You've come for a sad reason," he went on. "Things are about to change. Poor Janet. This will be hard on her. I won't live to see the sunrise."

"No," she said quickly. "You can't talk like that. You have no reason to. It's cruel to scare your wife like this. If you believe something that isn't true, you need to fight it, or at least stop saying it out loud. You're not well—I can tell just by looking at you. But I'm sure you'll feel much better tomorrow, and even better the day after that."

"I'm not sick, Maud," he said. "Feel my pulse if you don't believe me. No fever, nothing wrong. I've never felt healthier. But still, I know that before that clock strikes five, I'll be dead."

Lady Walsingham felt afraid—and that fear made her angry.

"I've already told you what I think," she said firmly. "It's wrong to scare Janet like this with your strange ideas. Look at the facts—there's no reason at all for you to believe this. How can you be so heartless to someone who loves you this much and actually believes what you say?"

"Enough, Maud. There's nothing to argue about. If I'm still here tomorrow, then you can say all of this again. But now, go back to Janet. She needs you. I hate to see her in pain, and I only told her because I didn't want her caught off guard. Please do everything you can to help her stay calm. What's done is done."

He paused, staring at her like he was thinking about saying more. But whatever was on his mind, he decided to keep it to himself.

Then he let go of her hand, turned quickly, and walked away.

Chapter XXIX.
Dr. Torvey's Opinion

When Lady Walsingham got to the top of the stairs, her maid told her that Lady Mardykes was downstairs in the same room. As she walked closer, she heard her sister Mary's voice and found them together. Mary couldn't sleep, so she got dressed again and came downstairs to be with Janet.

The room looked much more welcoming now. Candles were lit, a warm fire burned in the fireplace, and a tea set sat on a small table near the hearth. The two sisters were talking, and Lady Mardykes seemed calmer. They were alone in the room.

"Did you see him, Maud?" Lady Mardykes asked right away, hurrying to her as soon as she walked in.

"Yes, I did," Maud replied. "I talked to him, and—"

"Well?" Janet cut in.

"And I still feel the same," Maud said. "He told me he isn't sick, and I really think he's just anxious. You know how men are when something's bothering them—stubborn and dramatic. I think once the time he's so worried about passes without anything happening, we'll all realize this was just in his head."

"Oh, Maud, I wish I could believe you!" Janet cried. "If I could only be sure you really do think there's still hope. Please, Maud, be honest—what do you really think?"

Lady Walsingham was caught off guard by the question.

"Come on now, you can't let yourself get carried away," she said gently. "We're all just reacting to the serious way he's behaving. But people often believe their own fears—that's not unusual."

"Oh, Maud," Janet sobbed, "you don't really believe it. You're only saying that to make me feel better. You have no hope—none at all!" She broke down again, hiding her face in her hands.

Lady Walsingham stayed quiet for a moment. Then, putting a hand on her sister's arm, she said, "Look, Janet, there's no point in me repeating the same things. In just a few hours, we'll know who was right. Try to calm down and pull yourself together. My maid told me you sent for Doctor Torvey. You can't let him see you like this—he'll think something terrible is going on. Unless you plan to tell him about Bale's prediction—and we both know what kind of story that would start spreading around Golden Friars. I think I hear him coming now."

And sure enough, Doctor Torvey walked in with the serious look of someone who had just finished a bottle of port and a few glasses of sherry but still wanted to act respectful in front of the ladies. He bowed and waited to be addressed.

"Please sit, Doctor Torvey," Lady Walsingham said politely, taking charge since her sister was too upset. "My sister, Lady Mardykes, has gotten it into her head that something's wrong with Sir Bale. I just spoke with him. He doesn't look great, but he says he's fine. Do you think he's alright? I mean, perfectly well?"

The doctor cleared his throat and gave a slightly tipsy speech about Sir Bale's health. His conclusion? There was nothing seriously wrong. If anything, Sir Bale just needed to live more like a typical country gentleman, and he'd be as healthy as anyone else.

"At most," he added, slurring a bit, "maybe a little quinine—nothing more. He's really in very sound health."

Lady Walsingham nodded at her sister, trying to reassure her.

"I've been sent for, Lady Walsingham," he continued, chuckling. "Old Jack Amerald overdid it with the port again—feels a bit strange in the stomach, poor fellow. I've done what I can here, so I'll be off now. Just a bit of snow and some cold air—that's all."

After more comments about the weather and their long trip, Doctor Torvey politely said goodbye and left. A few moments later, they heard the sound of his gig's wheels and the muffled clopping of his horse in the snowy courtyard.

Outside, only a few snowflakes were falling, sometimes stopping completely before starting again. The moonlight was bright, and the landscape glowed white under its shine. No one had closed the curtain on the large window, and Lady Walsingham thought the light had grown harsher. Snakes Island looked closer, its bare tree limb raised like an arm reaching out. It reminded her of something dark and threatening.

Everything familiar now seemed cold and eerie in the bright moonlight. The sisters fell silent, and a feeling of fear and suspense filled the room. Lady Mardykes kept standing up to listen at the door, hoping for a sound or a voice, but hearing nothing. The heavy feeling only grew stronger, and more than an hour passed in that strange, tense quiet.

Chapter XXX.
Hush!

Pale and quiet, the three sisters sat together. The room was filled with a heavy silence, thick with fear. Lady Mardykes looked calm, but it was the kind of calm that comes when you're too overwhelmed to react.

Then, without warning, Sir Bale Mardykes entered the room silently. The moonlight on the floor lit up his face in a way that almost made him look like he was smiling. He lifted a finger to his lips, signaling them not to speak. He gently took the hands of his two sisters-in-law, then leaned over his wife, who was barely conscious, and kissed her cold forehead twice. Without saying a word, he turned and left the room just as quietly.

For a few moments, no one moved. Then Lady Walsingham grabbed a candle from the table and followed after him. From the hallway, she saw him reach the top of the stairs, turn the corner, and continue up to the next floor with a candle in hand.

Nervous and curious, she followed from a distance. She watched him enter his private room and close the door behind him. She crept up to the door, heart pounding, and listened.

She heard him pacing for a while. Then came the sound of someone dropping onto a bed. Silence followed. Her sisters joined her a moment later. She motioned for them to stay quiet.

Lady Haworth stood behind them, whispering a prayer, hands tightly clasped. Lady Mardykes leaned against the doorframe, pale and silent. Lady Walsingham kept listening. One minute passed. Then another. Still nothing. Her anxiety grew. She grabbed the doorknob and turned it sharply, but the door was locked. A soft voice from inside said, "Hush, hush!"

More frightened now, she knocked hard. No answer. She knocked again, harder, shaking the door with all her strength. The fear on her face must have been clear because Lady Mardykes suddenly screamed and collapsed to the floor.

Servants came running at the sound. They carried Lady Mardykes to her room, with Lady Haworth at her side. Meanwhile, the others forced the door open. Inside, they found Sir Bale lying on the bed.

He was dead. His body was cold and stiff. The man who once ruled Mardykes Hall was gone.

Today, there's a marble monument for him in the church at Golden Friars, near the altar. It shows Sir Bale carved in stone, dressed in old-style clothes from 1770. An inscription praises his life, written by his grieving widow, Lady Mardykes.

Lady Walsingham had wanted to soften some of the overly dramatic parts, which people in town quietly laughed at—but now no one says a word. What truly mattered was the deep love behind it, the way his wife saw him through loving eyes.

A few days after the funeral, Lady Mardykes left the Hall for good. She spent the rest of her life mostly with Lady Walsingham and died in 1790. She was buried beside her husband in Golden Friars.

Sir Bale had inherited the estate with no conditions. He had started thinking about a will, but never finished it. Because he died with no will or children, a part of their marriage contract gave everything to Lady Mardykes.

In her will, she left it all to William Feltram—her cousin and also a distant relative of Sir Bale—on the condition that he take the Mardykes name and use their family crest, though the Feltram symbol would still be included.

So, in the end, Philip Feltram's prediction came true: the Mardykes estate did end up in Feltram hands.

In 1795, the baronet title was brought back. William Feltram became Sir William Mardykes and held the title for fifteen years.

The End

Thank You for Reading

Dear Reader,

We hope this timeless classic has sparked your imagination and enriched your literary journey. Now that you've turned the final page, we want to share a vision for the future of reading—one where every classic you've ever wanted to explore is at your fingertips, in a format that best suits your life.

We'd like to invite you to gain immediate, unlimited digital & audiobook access to hundreds of the most treasured literary classics ever written—along with the option to secure deluxe paperback, hardcover & box set editions at printing cost. Together, we can spark a new global literary renaissance alongside our small, independent publishing house called "The Library of Alexandria."

Thousands of years ago, the Library of Alexandria stood as a beacon of knowledge—until it was lost to history. We aim to reignite that spirit of preservation and discovery right now, in the modern age—only this time, it's accessible to all, in every language and every format.

Picture a world where every timeless classic, novel, poem, or philosophical treatise is not only available to read but also updated for today's readers—modernized, translated into any language or dialect, and ready to enjoy in any format you choose, whether that is in an eBook, audiobook, paperback, or deluxe hardcover & box set version a printing cost.

By joining our movement to rebuild the modern Library of Alexandria, you become part of an unprecedented mission to offer:

- **Unlimited Audiobook & eBook Access to the Greatest Classics of All Time**

  Instantly explore thousands of legendary works, from Plato and Shakespeare to Jane Austen and Leo Tolstoy. All are instantly ready to read or listen to, giving you a complete literary universe at your fingertips.

- **Paperback & Deluxe Editions at Printing Costs:**

  Purchase any title in a paperback, deluxe hardbound, or deluxe boxset edition at printing costs, shipped right to your doorstep. Curate your personal library of Alexandria with editions worthy of display—crafted to last, designed to captivate, and delivered straight to your door.

- **Modern translations for Contemporary Readers in all languages and dialects**

  Discover a vast selection of classics reimagined in clear, current language—no more struggling with outdated phrases or obscure references. Next to the original versions, we aim to offer translations in as many languages and dialects as possible.

  As we continue our translation efforts and add new languages, readers everywhere can connect with these works as if they were written today. By bridging linguistic divides, you're contributing to ensuring that these timeless stories become more meaningful, accessible, and inspiring for people across the globe.

- **Your Personal Library of Alexandria:**

  Over the months and years, you'll curate a unique physical archive of classics—each volume a testament to your taste, curiosity, and love of knowledge. It's not just about owning books—it's about curating a cultural legacy you'll cherish and pass down for generations to come.

- **Join a Global Literary Renaissance:**

  Your support fuels an ongoing mission: allowing us to reinvest in offering deluxe print editions (including special boxsets) at their true cost, broaden the range of available formats and translations, and extend the reach of these works to new audiences worldwide. By joining today, you're not just preserving a legacy of masterpieces; you set in motion a powerful wave of literary accessibility.

  We are more than a publisher—we're a movement, and we can't do it alone. Your support lets us scale our mission, preserving and reimagining history's greatest works for tomorrow's readers.

Become a Torchbearer of knowledge.

Thank you for picking up this book and allowing us into your literary journey. As you turn the pages, know that you're part of something larger: a global effort to keep these stories alive, share their wisdom across borders and generations, and spark a true cultural revival for the modern era.

If this resonates with you—please consider taking the next step by visiting:

www.libraryofalexandria.com

With gratitude and a shared love of knowledge,

The Modern Library of Alexandria Team

Visit:

www.libraryofalexandria.com

Or scan the code below:

www.ingramcontent.com/pod-product-compliance
Lightning Source LLC
Chambersburg PA
CBHW011356010726
47494CB00008B/2336